"Let Me Go!" She Demanded.

For answer, he put his hand low on her back and pulled her toward him.

"Is this pretense, Carrie?" he whispered, bending his face toward her, his eyes searching hers.

"No—No, no—" It was all she managed to breathe out before he set his mouth on hers. The next moment she was swept up in his arms and he was carrying her across the room, his feet silent on the thick carpet.

"No!" she gasped again.

"Why not?" he asked harshly. She could feel the rasp of his chin against her tender skin, his lips caressing her cheek. A treacherous weakness overcame her. . . .

DOROTHY CORK

was born in Australia and has lived there most of her life. Her many readers may well have guessed this, as her entertaining novels are frequently set in her native land. Not that she limits herself to this region. She is an enthusiastic and perceptive traveler. Her whole-hearted enjoyment of life is reflected in her lively romances.

Dear Reader:

At Silhouette we try to publish books with you, our reader, in mind, and we're always trying to think of something new. We're very pleased to announce the creation of Silhouette First Love, a new line of contemporary romances written by the very finest young adult writers especially for our twelve-to-sixteen-year-old readers. First Love has many of the same elements you've enjoyed in Silhouette Romances—love stories, happy endings and the same attention to detail and description—but features heroines and situations with which our younger readers can more easily identify.

First Love from Silhouette will be available in bookstores this October. We will introduce First Love with six books, and each month thereafter we'll bring you two new First Love romances.

We welcome any suggestions or comments, and I invite you to write to us at the address below.

Karen Solem
Editor-in-Chief
Silhouette Books
P.O. Box 769
New York, N.Y. 10019

DOROTHY CORK
By Honour Bound

Silhouette Romance

Published by Silhouette Books New York

America's Publisher of Contemporary Romance

Other Silhouette Romances by Dorothy Cork

Secret Marriage

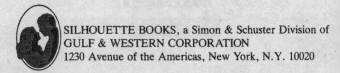

SILHOUETTE BOOKS, a Simon & Schuster Division of
GULF & WESTERN CORPORATION
1230 Avenue of the Americas, New York, N.Y. 10020

Copyright © 1981 by Dorothy Cork

Distributed by Pocket Books

ISBN: 0-671-57103-6

First Silhouette printing September, 1981

10 9 8 7 6 5 4 3 2 1

America's Publisher of Contemporary Romance

Printed in the U.S.A.

By Honour Bound

Chapter One

Caroline Adams turned the key in the lock and pushed open the door of her small flat in North Sydney. Switching on the wall lamp, she flung herself down on the divan that at night became her bed, and let the tears run down her cheeks, tears that she'd been holding back ever since Paul had said so casually an hour or so ago, "Listen Carrie, will you mind very much if we forget our little dream of starting up a catering business together?"

She had blinked with shock and felt herself go rigid. What did he mean? Forget the catering business? Or all the rest of it as well, the whole relationship? He couldn't mean that, of course, and she pulled herself together and looked at him across the table they were sharing in the city restaurant.

They had both just completed a three year course at the Catering College, and were having dinner together. To celebrate, Carrie had thought happily. She hadn't seen a great deal of Paul during the last few months. He had been working in a hotel, and Carrie had worked part time in a restaurant, a position she had now given up because of the plans she and Paul had made to start out on their own. He was twenty-six, and she, more than five years younger, had been depending on his experience and maturity to guide them.

She had asked him cautiously, "Do you have something better in mind, Paul? I don't mind changing. You're the brains in this combination and of course I'll go along with whatever you say."

He had glanced away from her, not answering her hesitant smile. Their relationship had been strained all evening, ever since they'd met outside Wynyard Station and he'd brought her here to eat. She'd been babbling away about the relief of finishing with study—the bliss of not having to work night after night in the restaurant, but he, she saw now, had been very quiet.

She fiddled with the stem of her wine glass and asked him steadily, "What are you trying to tell me, Paul? We're still going into something together, aren't we?"

He looked into her dark, black-lashed eyes, then away again, and grimaced.

"Oh heavens—I feel really mean about this, Carrie but—no, I don't think so." He reached for the carafe and topped up both their glasses. "Something I just can't afford to miss has come up for me."

"But not for me?" she put in when he stopped, and felt her heart beating nervously fast.

"Well, once we get it all going we could probably fit you in."

"We?" she repeated. "Who do you mean, Paul? Tell me."

"This girl I've met. And her father," he said, and she saw a nerve move in his jaw even while her own heart froze. A girl, another girl.

"Go on," she said, swallowing and hearing how her voice shook.

He must have heard it, too, but his face hardened rather than otherwise. "Her name's Josie Tanner," he said, "and I met her about three months ago. Her father's buying a little restaurant and he wants us to run it. Me and Josie." He looked at Carrie uneasily. "All this has only just happened, Carrie. I haven't been hiding it from you, you're the first to know. I'm seeing Frank Tanner tomorrow, and we'll go into it all in depth. It's a tremendous opportunity, you must admit, one I couldn't possibly pass up. You and I would have been struggling, Carrie, and whether you know it or not, that five-thousand-dollar legacy you're expecting when you turn twenty-one would vanish without a trace, like a soap bubble. It would take that and all my savings to set the thing on its legs, and they'd be pretty shaky legs at that. As it is, you'll be able to hang onto your money and well, something marvellous is sure to turn up for you. If it doesn't, you can always come to Josie and Paul's and—"

He had stopped. Carrie felt the tears ready to flow, but she drank some wine and tried to get control over her madly whirling thoughts. She wanted to burst into tears, and as well she wanted to protest loudly and volubly. She wanted to exclaim angrily, and she wanted to beseech him, "You can't let it end like this, Paul. I've been dreaming about it for two years, ever since we worked together in the college kitchen and you said what a flair I had for food presentation, and how about we'd get together and cater for parties and dinners and celebrations. And ever since you first kissed me and said we'd get married and be a husband and wife team, really old-fashioned. I've been living for that, I haven't been out with other guys, I've been happy because—"

"You must hate me," Paul said, looking down at the table.

"I don't hate you. How can you think I'd change as quickly as that?" she said bitterly. "Are you—are you going to marry this girl, this Josie Tanner—in the good old-fashioned way?"

"Well, yes," he said a little sullenly. "Her father wouldn't be helping us along otherwise."

"Don't tell me you're doing it because of that," she said with a laugh that was half a sob. "What's she like? Is she pretty?"

"I guess so. Different from you. Tallish, blonde, blue-eyed. Elegant. Older than you, almost my age. A bit spoilt, I suppose."

Carrie drank the rest of her wine. Spoilt. Had she told her wealthy father, "I want Paul Stanhope," and he'd said, "Right, darling, I'll buy you a restaurant, you can marry him and run it together and live happily ever after?" She looked at Paul through her lashes. He was good-looking, a little arrogant, with a high-bridged nose, greenish eyes and brown hair that was always perfectly groomed. Did he love Josie Tanner? Or was it just that he couldn't afford to miss such an opportunity? Her own little offering of five thousand dollars had faded into oblivion. She couldn't compete with a girl whose father was obviously loaded. Her own father had died in England when she was four, and she and her mother had come out to Australia to be with her mother's only relatives, her two sisters, Carrie's Aunt Lena and Aunt Janet, her cousin Kim's mother.

"Well, I hope you'll be happy, Paul," she said after a moment. She felt slightly sick and wasn't sure if it was the wine or the death of her hopes. *What on earth am I going to do now?* she asked herself wildly.

"Something marvellous will turn up for you," Paul said. But—*what?* It didn't seem very probable *she'd* meet some man whose father wanted to set them up in business. And she didn't want to. Nor did she want to go back to the restaurant.

She sat staring at her glass and Paul drank his wine and said nothing for at least three minutes. Then he asked her almost accusingly, "What will you do, Carrie?"

She shrugged. She wondered what she looked like. She could feel a spot of colour burning high in each cheek, and she ran slender fingers through her thick dark brown hair and wished futilely that she wasn't wearing this ridiculous white cotton jersey dress, printed all over with the words LOVE, ETERNAL and HAPPINESS. Paul hadn't commented on it, and now she knew why.

So what *would* she do? She pushed back the dark hair from her ears, where earrings dangled, earrings he had given her last Christmas, with little stars made of simulated diamonds, as she told him slowly, "Maybe I'll go up to Queensland. My cousin Kim's a receptionist at a hotel there, on the Gold Coast. Well, you know that already. I might get something there, too. I don't know. I'll have to think about it."

"It sounds like a good idea," he said sounding relieved. "Well, have you had all you want?"

"I've had more than I want," she said wryly. She stood up and smoothed her dress down over her slender hips.

"Now don't be bitter, Carrie," he reproached her. "All that nonsense we talked, it was more or less to fill in time, to keep us going, wasn't it?"

"Was it? Well, *I* believed in it," she said. "And in you," she added under her breath.

"We'll keep in touch anyhow," he said. "I want to know what happens to you, I truly do. And I hope it's something marvellous."

Carrie moved ahead of him toward the street door. How can anything marvellous happen to you when quite suddenly the man you're in love with tells you he's teaming up with someone else?

"I'll probably meet a millionaire or something," she said, feeling suffocated. "The Gold Coast must abound in elderly millionaires. I might even marry one. Wouldn't *that* be marvellous?"

"Carrie—don't sound so cynical!" He grabbed her arm as they emerged into the street. "Look, I'll see you home."

"I'd rather you didn't."

"Why not?"

"Oh, Paul, why do you think? Josie Tanner wouldn't like it."

"Please yourself then," he said shortly and added more gently, "I'll ring you tomorrow, Carrie. If I hear of anything going that might suit you, I'll let you know."

She nodded and turned her face away from him, tears in her eyes.

Back in the privacy of her tiny flat, she lay on the divan and gave way to tears. Her whole future had disappeared. Paul didn't love her enough to stick with her—he couldn't miss the chance that was being handed to him on a plate by another girl's father. Carrie put her hands over her face and wept. . . .

She'd dried her eyes and was trying to pull herself together when the telephone rang. She leapt up. It was Paul! He'd changed his mind and everything was going to be all right.

It wasn't Paul, of course. It was her cousin Kim on a long-distance line.

"Carrie? It's Kim, here. How are things?"

Oh, things were fabulous, they were brilliant! Carrie said, "They're fine. I've passed my exams and I've finished up at the restaurant. Now I can take it easy for a bit before I—"

"Oh good," Kim interrupted. "I hoped you wouldn't be working tonight. I've been trying to get you and I thought you must be out somewhere with Paul. Is he, er, there with you now?"

"No, he's not," Carrie said and was amazed at her own calmness. "I guess I didn't tell you, Paul and I have called it off."

"Good lord! Then what about the catering business you were talking about?"

"That's off, too," Carrie said.

"Really?" Kim didn't ask questions or even offer sympathy, or enquire if it was needed. In fact, the way she said Really? sounded almost as if she were relieved. "Then listen—can you come up here to Surfers Paradise? Right away, I mean. Tomorrow?"

Tomorrow! Carrie was slightly stunned. She didn't want to go to Queensland tomorrow. Paul was going to ring her and it might be silly, but she couldn't help hoping that by some miracle he'd have changed his mind about those beastly Tanners. . . .

"Not as soon as that, Kim," she said. "I mean, how can I? I'd have to pack—fix everything up. Besides—*why?*"

"Of course you can!" Kim explained, ignoring Carrie's last question completely. "Ring TAA or Ansett tonight—you're sure to get a flight some time tomorrow. And you won't need to pack much—the weather's gorgeous here, and you needn't stay long."

Carrie laughed incredulously. "I'm not coming a thousand kilometres just to stay with you for a couple of days, Kim. It costs too much for that and besides, I've been thinking of looking for work on the Gold Coast. What's the big hurry, anyhow?"

There was silence for a moment then Kim said shakily, "I'm in a mess, Carrie, an awful mess. You've got to come—*please.*"

There was a note of desperation in her voice and Carrie asked quickly, "What sort of a mess, Kim?"

"I—I can't tell you over the phone. I'll explain it all when you're here. But you must help me—promise you'll come, Carrie. Promise."

"I—all right, of course I will," Carrie said helplessly.

"Oh, I knew you would! Come straight to the flat—it's my day off and I'll be there. Okay?"

"Okay," Carrie repeated.

"You're a darling! I'll see you tomorrow then. Good-bye."

"Good-bye," Carrie echoed. She put the receiver back on its cradle, her own problems temporarily banished from her mind. She had a strong suspicion that the mess Kim was in would be concerned with money, and even while she rang one of the air companies and arranged her flight, part of her mind was busy worrying about her cousin.

They'd grown up as closely as sisters, for Carrie's mother had died less than a year after they arrived in Sydney. After that, she lived with Aunt Janet, Uncle Jack and Kim, who was her elder by a year. It was a long time before Carrie understood that Kim's father was a compulsive gambler, and a constant drain on his wife, who worked in an advertizing agency in the city. Uncle Jack had once been a schoolteacher, but he'd had a breakdown of some kind, and when he was over it, he hadn't gone back to teaching but had settled down to write a book. Carrie had no idea what it was about, for it never materialised. He spent most of his time on the racecourse, or out with his friends. It was hardly a happy family life for either Kim or Carrie, and Kim had come out of it badly, feeling herself unloved and insecure. Her father died of a heart attack just before the girls, who were in the same year despite the difference between their ages, left school, and though they both gained places at the College of Catering Studies, Kim failed her exams and had to drop out. Aunt Janet soon married again, a man named Roger Warner, whom she had known for years, and who wasn't interested in burdening himself with stepdaughters. They had gone to live in New Zealand and neither Kim nor Carrie ever heard from them. Which meant that Kim had no one to turn to but Carrie when she was in trouble.

Having booked her flight to Coolangatta for the following day, Carrie began to pack her suitcase and to tidy the flat, and while she was doing that she came across a cutting she'd taken from the social pages of a magazine a couple of days ago, meaning to post it off to Kim. It was about Steve Revellion, Kim's boss. Not her immediate boss. That was the manager of the Daystar Hotel. Steve Revellion was a director of Revellion-West Enterprises, which owned hotels all round Australia, and had also ventured most successfully into real estate development.

Carrie read the article again with a vague interest that was deliberately encouraged, so as to prevent herself from dwelling on her own problems. She didn't want to start thinking of Paul Stanhope again and arrive in Surfers Paradise looking a sight, her eyes swollen from crying.

"Our reporter managed to have a few words with the elusive Steve Revellion, in Sydney for a conference this week," she read. "This man is a real-estate developer with a difference—he's really concerned about the environment. 'There'll be no high rise buildings on property recently acquired by Revellion-West on the Queensland coast,' he said firmly. Asked whether it was true he intended stepping down from his top position with Revellion-West Enterprises, and spending more time at Quaama Springs, his thriving beef cattle property on the Darling Downs, he refused to be pinned down. 'I never discuss my plans before they're fully formulated,' he said. He has figured amongst Australia's most eligible bachelors for several years and has proved himself a far from easy mark for husband hunters. But rumour has it that wedding bells will soon bring to a close his hectic life of ruling his far-flung empire that extends from Sydney across to Perth. But that is another topic that he refused to discuss—in the most charming way."

One of those millionaires she'd joked about to Paul, Carrie thought with a stab at her heart. Well, she wasn't likely ever to meet *him.* She doubted whether Kim, in her role of junior receptionist, would move in circles that would touch his.

But Kim, she was to discover very soon, had a lot more dealings with Steve Revellion than she could ever have imagined in her wildest dreams.

From Coolangatta, the next afternoon, Carrie took the coach north along the Gold Coast with its thirty-five kilometres of golden beaches and jewel-coloured surf. It was not yet December, but the holiday makers were there in their thousands, though there were still plenty of quiet, almost deserted strips of sand. The Daystar Hotel where Kim worked was at fashionable Surfers Paradise, and leaving the coach on the highway, which passed through the centre of the town, Carrie walked to the two-storey block of flats where Kim lived. The sun was blazingly hot though the afternoon was nearly over, but there was a cool breeze blowing in from the ocean, and Carrie's suitcase was not all that heavy. She had sensibly worn open sandals and a cool violet-coloured cotton dress with a white trim.

She had been here only once before, just after Kim moved north, and as her cousin let her into the flat she commented, "Kim! You've been redecorating! It's sumptuous."

Kim gave a pale smile and pushed her long golden hair back from a face that was a little plump and still oddly childish. Her eyes looked faintly pink as if she had been crying, and her smile vanished as her lower lip began to tremble. Instead of replying to Carrie's comment, she said nervously, "Well, come on in,

17

anyhow. I've made up your bed and pushed my things along in the wardrobe so you can hang some of your dresses up. I guess you'd like something to drink before we begin to talk."

"Just fruit juice will do," Carrie said, aware of her cousin's emotional state.

There was only one bedroom in the flat, but it was equipped with twin beds, and Carrie opened her suitcase and began to unpack. She'd spent most of the flight north thinking about Paul. She was desperately hurt by his behaviour. She'd thought they had such a good understanding, that she could trust him, believe in him. It had never occurred to her that their plans would come to nothing. She would have staked her life on their materialising, because they'd discussed the whole project in detail—how they'd finance the business, if they needed to borrow money, what kind of clientele they'd set out to attract, the sort of food they'd specialise in. Carrie had an exercise book almost filled with ideas she'd collected over the past two years, and if Paul hadn't talked much about their marriage for a while, it hadn't bothered her, he, like herself, took it for granted. That was how she saw it. She knew they'd have a quiet, no-fuss wedding not only because she had no family, but also because they were practical people.

But Paul had proved to be even more practical than she had suspected. He couldn't pass up a good opportunity.

Oh, Paul, she thought with inward anguish as she shook out a dress and hung it in Kim's overcrowded wardrobe. *How could you? How could you? And not to know how I'd feel—to ask me would it matter very much if we forgot our little dream?*

18

She longed to hate him for being so unfeeling, but she couldn't. Was this what happened at the end of a love affair? You were a mixture of emotional tears, and of cold, cold disbelief—not just in him, but in everything, in the whole world.

Kim came to the door. "Come on, Carrie. I've mixed some punch and I've got to tell you what's happened."

Carrie brought her mind back to the present and to Kim with a bang. Maybe Kim's troubles were worse than her own, and she hoped there was more chance of helping Kim that there would be of Kim's helping her. She left her half-unpacked luggage and followed her cousin into the living room, sat down in a linen covered armchair, and accepted the tall, fluted, expensive-looking punch glass that Kim offered her. Wide windows looked across a tiny balcony towards a row of flats on the other side of the street. Behind them was another street, and then the Esplanade and the beach. Kim had decorated her living room with big pots of indoor plants and it was cool and green and pleasant.

Kim sat down on the couch and Carrie looked at her expectantly.

"What's this mess you're in, Kim?" She gestured with one hand at the well-furnished room, the expensive-looking ornaments, the paintings on the wall. "Have you been spending too much money?"

Kim nodded and bit her lip, then suddenly burst into tears.

Carrie put her glass down on the low polished table and went to sit beside her cousin, and to put an arm around her shoulders.

"Come on now, Kim, don't cry. Just tell me all

about it and we'll see what we can do. Is it really bad?"

Kim blew her nose and sobbed out, "Worse than you could ever imagine. I've—I've had a threatening letter from the finance company—I could go to gaol. Carrie—I've been desperate—sick with worrying about it all—crying myself to sleep—not knowing who to turn to. My mother—I've scarcely heard a word from her since she and that mean husband of hers went to New Zealand. There's—there's only you."

"How much money do you owe?" Carrie asked carefully when Kim finally spluttered to a stop. Her mind went rapidly to her own bank account. Her savings were not very considerable what with the expenses connected with her study, the flat and everyday living costs.

Kim's blue eyes, swollen with tears, looked at her, and she said in a small voice, "Nearly six thousand dollars."

Carrie stared, appalled. Kim had got into debt once before when she'd been unhappy. She'd rushed around spending money, and then tried to win it back on the horses. Her stepfather had come to her rescue, most unwillingly, on that occasion, and he'd warned her that if it ever happened again he didn't want to know. She'd had to pay back every penny of it when she turned twenty-one and received her legacy from Aunt Lena, a legacy that was tied up firmly and was completely untouchable, as was Carrie's, until her twenty-first birthday. A precaution taken, by Aunt Lena, as a protection against Kim's profligate father, Carrie suspected.

"How on earth did you get through all that money, Kim?" she asked at last.

Kim shook her head miserably. "I don't know, Carrie. Things for the flat, clothes, little gifts. It's when I'm lonely or unhappy, and I just seem to feel better if I—if I go out and spend money. And then I overspend and I do a bit of gambling. I've won good money at the races, but I've been unlucky lately, that's all."

"But, Kim, I thought you were happy here. What about that man you told me about last time you wrote, Gene Lennox?"

Kim shook her head. "It was before he took any notice of me. He was taking another girl out, and I didn't think I stood a chance. There was just no one. It's different now. I see a lot of him and I think he's serious, but I—I can't ask *him* to fork out six thousand dollars. It would be the end of everything if he even knew how silly I've been. I won't do it ever again, Carrie, I promise."

It was all very well promising, but Carrie was searching her mind feverishly to try to find a solution to Kim's dilemma. Finally she asked, "How long has the finance company given you to find the money, Kim? I don't turn twenty-one for another five weeks, and you know I can't get hold of that money any sooner."

"No, I know." A strangely guilty look had come into Kim's blue eyes, and she leaned back on the sofa and studied her pretty pink fingernails. "I only have five days left."

"Then how on earth did you think I could help you?" Carrie exclaimed, both worried and exasper-ated.

"Well, I—I haven't told you eveything yet," Kim said. "I've done something awful, I just don't know how to tell you."

"What have you done?" Carrie asked sharply.

Haltingly, the story came out.

Kim, it appeared, had been weeping over her plight at work, and Steve Revellion, of all people, had found her and asked what was the trouble.

"He just insisted I must tell him," Kim said. "He said I was a member of the staff at one of his hotels, and if I was in trouble then he wanted to know why."

"And you told him?"

Kim shook her head. "Not exactly. You see, I've sort of borrowed money from the desk a few times—not a lot and I've paid back most of it—but I was afraid he'd find out about it somehow if I told him the truth. And he's the kind of man who would sack you on the spot if he thought you weren't dependable. He has a reputation for being really hard, especially where women are concerned. And I guess it was because I was so scared that I—I told him a terrible lie."

She stopped and picked at the nail polish on her thumb, and Carrie said, "Well, what was the terrible lie?"

"Oh, you'll never forgive me, Carrie," Kim wailed. "I—I said I was upset about—about my cousin who was in debt and wanted me to help her and—and I didn't see how I could."

Carrie gasped. "Why on earth did you say that?"

"I—I don't know really. It just seemed to come into my head. After all, he's frightfully rich, and I didn't see why he shouldn't help. I don't want to go to gaol, you know."

"And did he offer to help?" Carrie asked tersely.

"Not exactly. He wanted to know how much you—I—owed, and I explained you had this legacy coming up and it was just that the finance company was so ruthless and wouldn't give you—me—time to pay. So," she took a deep breath, "he said he'd like to see you—that I'd better send you along to talk about it. Today. And that's why I rang you last night."

Carrie stared at her stupefied. "You mean I have to see Steve Revellion and—and talk about it? Honestly, Kim."

Kim put her hands to her face and began to cry. "Don't tell me you won't do it. I'll be sent to prison, Carrie—I'll lose my job, and Gene. My whole life will be ruined. You won't have to tell him anything much, it's only asking a little of you. I've explained. You might have to sign something saying you'll pay the money back when you're twenty-one, that's all, and then you need never see him again. And I'll pay you back, Carrie, I promise. I'll save like mad. I'll get the money somehow."

Carrie simmered down. Kim really was the limit. She might have needed the money herself, and she didn't have any illusions about Kim's refunding it in too much of a hurry. However, as it happened, she didn't need the money, and Kim seemed really scared she'd be sent to prison.

"All right," she said at last. "I'll go and see him. Tell me when and where—"

Kim brightened at once. "Between five and six this evening, in his flat at the hotel. It's on the fourteenth floor."

So soon! Carrie felt sick at the thought. That man she'd read about in the magazine column—he sounded so positive, so sure of himself, so intimidating. What on earth was she going to tell him? From what Kim had said about him, he was quite likely to tell her what he thought of her for her supposed extravagance, and refuse to help. *Well, after all, why should he help a stranger?* she asked herself reasonably. Still, for Kim's sake she must see what she could achieve. Somehow she must get that cheque from him—and sign away her legacy, just like that, as though it were nothing.

"I know you don't understand, Carrie," Kim said into her thoughts. "But, really, I just don't seem able to help it. It's like a sickness. And it's inherited. You know what my father was like. Nothing could keep him away from the racecourse. There was something wrong with his personal life, I guess, and I'm like that. When things go wrong, it seems as if I just have to go out and buy things. I saw a psychiatrist about it once. He said I'm insecure, and it's all tied up with the fact my parents didn't care about me. It's sort of compensation. If I'd kept going to him, he might have cured me, but it cost so much each visit, and I really thought I could manage by myself, once I understood. And then I just got worse and worse. It's different now, I'm going with Gene. I'll never do it again, honestly. If you'll just help me out this time, Carrie. I'd die if I had to go to gaol."

"Well, you won't have to go to gaol," Carrie said definitely. "I'll see that man, and if he won't help us out we'll have to think of something else, that's all."

"It's too late to think of something else," Kim said, tearful again. "The finance company gave me a week, and there are only five days left. You'll just have to persuade Steve Revellion. Maybe you should act repentant, really repentant, and explain it's just for a few weeks. He can't possibly refuse if he knows that. And I've told you that I'll scrape and save and pay it back."

"I know," Carrie said with a sigh. And Kim said

with unconscious cruelty, "Anyhow, it's not as if you needed it at once, now that it's all off between you and Paul Stanhope."

"No," Carrie said. She didn't want to talk about it. She got up from the sofa. "Well, if I'm to be really persuasive, I'd better freshen myself up, take a shower and—for heavens sake, what am I going to wear? I'm not used to meeting millionaires, and I wasn't expecting anything like this. I know dress is casual on the Gold Coast, but I don't want to turn up looking like Cinderella before the fairy godmother arrived. Or do you think that might be a good idea?" she added. "So he can see at a glance I'm right out of funds."

"You'd better look your best," Kim said, uncertain how to take her remark. "He does have a reputation for being hard and callous, not only in business but where women are concerned. But all the same, he's always seen about with really glamourous girls, even if they never last long. He was jilted once—right at the altar, so they say. And he's never trusted women since."

"Then it's a wonder you persuaded him to see me," Carrie said dryly. "How *did* you do it?"

Kim shrugged. "I was really in a state, and he probably calculates he gets more out of his employees if they're happy." She glanced at her watch. "You'd better get moving, Carrie. I'll look for something stunning for you to wear while you take a shower."

When Carrie set out to walk along the Esplanade to the Daystar Hotel some little while later, she was wearing one of her own outfits—a finely striped black and white cotton skirt, and a very feminine blouse in white voile, with a softly embroidered collar. Kim's things were too loose for her, and as well, though she hadn't admitted it to her cousin, they were too ostentatious, both in colour and in style. Deeply plunging necklines were not for Carrie who had small breasts, and lacked the rather luscious figure of her cousin.

Once at the hotel, she asked the receptionist, another junior of about eighteen she guessed, if she would let Mr. Revellion know she was there as he was expecting her. Half a minute later, she was told, "You're to go straight up, Miss Adams. It's the fourteenth floor."

In the lift, Carrie's legs began to shake and she looked at herself nervously in the mirror. She wasn't looking forward to this interview in the least, and not even her natural curiosity about the man could make her relax. He opened the door of the flat himself, and she felt her pulses begin to hammer. He was younger than she'd expected—still in his thirties, she thought—and far more formidable. Broad shouldered and muscular, with thick curling black hair, dark brows and an arrogant air. He wore light beige pants and a black shirt, unbuttoned far enough down to show the mat of dark hair on his chest. His eyes were of a vivid and startling blue, whose fire seemed to leap across the distance between them and scorch her, as he asked her to come inside.

With a murmured, "Thank you," Carrie moved past him and let herself into the room that opened off the entrance hall. It was carpeted in off-white, and its huge windows framed the sapphire of the sea, whose roar she could hear, clear and insistent, even above the drumming of blood in her ears.

He didn't asked her to sit down immediately, but

stood looking at her in silence for what seemed to Carrie to be an eternity. She stared back at him transfixed, aware of the mad hammering of her heart. Every rational thought seemed to have deserted her mind, so that she hardly knew why she was there, and was aware only of a sort of shattering male presence—and not a friendly one at that. She put an unsteady hand to her dark hair and touched her upper lip with her tongue. At least she had been trained at the College to walk and stand gracefully, and she was thankful for that now.

His head was tilted back a little as he studied her through those narrowed and stunningly blue eyes. She felt it almost physically as his gaze made a deliberate journey over her, from her dark shining hair to her flushed cheeks and thickly lashed eyes, then to her slight figure, the small pointed breasts only discreetly hinted at beneath the fine white blouse. Having taken in her black and white skirt and her white sandals, his gaze flicked quickly back to her face and he said, "So you're the spendthrift cousin who had one of my junior receptionists in tears. I'd never have guessed it. . . . Well, sit down, Miss Adams. I want to hear about this desperate fix you're in. Kim seemed afraid you were about to be carried screaming off to prison at any moment, but you don't look like a girl who's expecting the fall of the axe to me."

Carrie said nothing, she was still too stunned. *This is crazy,* she thought as she sank into the chair he indicated—a comfortable armchair, upholstered in pale brown suede. Kim had said she wouldn't have to talk much, just sign an IOU and wait for the cheque to be written, but she strongly suspected there was going to be a lot more to it than that, and the thought made her irritable. It really wasn't fair of Kim to let her in for this.

He waited a few seconds before he sat down, and Carrie looked at him from under her lashes. His head was tilted haughtily, and his broad shoulders and narrow hips were emphasised against the chalk white walls. The big room seemed to be a combination of private sitting room and of conference room, with its two long lounges, three armchairs and scattering of straight-backed chairs. There was a glass-fronted cocktail cabinet, a handsome bookcase, a narrow leather-topped table that could be a desk, and several low tables holding ashtrays and magazines. It was, she decided, a room used for conferences, for business meetings. This was a business meeting of course. There was nothing in the least personal about it. Caroline Adams wanted a loan, and she had to make a case for herself.

He sat down at last on one of the long sofas and she said reluctantly, "I thought Kim had explained everything."

"Then you thought wrong," he said coolly. "Kim was far too busy weeping to be coherent, and that, in fact, is the only reason I told her I'd see you. I did however get the idea you owed a considerable sum of money—considerable that is for a young girl—and that you were in danger of being thrown into gaol unless somebody came to the rescue." He settled back in the sofa and subjected her again to that unnerving scrutiny. "If you tell me the exact position, Miss Adams, I may be able to give you some advice."

Carrie's blood froze. He was going to give her some advice, and that was all. Kim had been indulging heavily in wishful thinking to imagine he was all set to hand out a cheque for six thousand dollars. And heavens! she was going to have to "confess" to being in debt to that extent—she who had never been in debt in her life.

She took a deep breath and tried to think clearly and logically, in some way that would get through to a hard-headed, unsentimental man with eyes so blue they hurt, but had not a vestige of friendliness or sympathy in them.

She said at last, "I'm in debt, Mr. Revellion. I owe some money to a finance company." She named it. "I have five days as from now to pay it back. It's about six thousand dollars and if I don't find it in that time, they're going to take action." She stopped and swallowed. His look had hardened if anything, and she had the terrible feeling that she didn't sound as if she were telling the truth. She hurried on, "I have a legacy coming to me when I turn twenty one, in about five weeks time. Once I receive that I'll be in the clear, I can pay back all I owe. The trouble is, the finance company won't give me any more time."

"So what do you expect me to do about it, Miss Adams?" he asked. Carrie gritted her teeth. Then she widened her eyes and smiled at him.

"I don't expect you to do anything, Mr. Revellion. I wasn't even aware of your existence until today. It was Kim who told me you'd agreed to see me, and I think just now you said, very generously, that you'd give me some advice."

His eyes glittered angrily and she knew she shouldn't have spoken like that. Still, she objected to eating dirt, and she hadn't asked his help. In fact, she didn't need help from him or from anyone else, though Kim did.

"You're not greatly addicted to the truth, are

you?" he said icily. "I'm already aware you asked Kim to see if I'd help you out, that you insisted she should do so, in fact." Carrie opened her mouth to tell him that wasn't true, then closed it again. There was no point in making a liar of Kim, and she'd only get herself into a mess anyhow.

"The advice I'm very much inclined to give you," he went on, "is to see your solicitor—if you have one. The one who's administering the estate from which you're to receive your legacy should do admirably. He can surely come to some arrangement with your creditors. What's the amount you expect to receive, by the way?"

Carrie felt herself blush deeply at something in his tone. It told her more clearly than words could have that he didn't believe she had any money coming to her at all—and he'd already said she wasn't addicted to the truth.

"I'm not allowed to borrow on it," she said stiffly. "That's a—a strict condition in the terms of my aunt's will." She knew, but wasn't going to tell him, that it was an attempt to make sure Kim's father wouldn't get hold of the money. "I'm not sure of the amount. It was five thousand, but of course some interest will have accrued, and I do have a little money of my own."

"No doubt bringing it conveniently up to just the amount you need to get yourself out of the mess you're in."

"That's right," Carrie said angrily. She wanted to spring to her feet and tell him to forget it and walk out. But she forced herself to think of Kim, even though she was furious with her for getting her into this ridiculous situation.

He said nothing more for five seconds. Then he

asked, "And just how do you come to owe so much money, Miss Adams?"

The sixty-four-dollar question. Carrie searched wildly in her mind. She had mad ideas of inventing an invalid mother, a little brother to support, anything. But she had a strong suspicion that in spite of anything he'd said, Kim had babbled out a lot of details which, even if they were incoherent, would have given him the general idea. Finally she said resignedly, "It's gradually accumulated. It—it just happens. I'm a compulsive spender, I suppose. Buy things on credit and then, my salary, my pay packet —doesn't cover it."

"And you're a gambler, aren't you? Or did I mistake what Kim said?"

Oh, I'm sure you didn't mistake what Kim said, Carrie thought bitterly. *Kim would have said it all—and you're pretending you understood nothing, just to put me through the mangle.*

Aloud, she told him, "Yes, I'm a gambler. It's a weakness I've inherited," she added for good measure. "But I suppose Kim said something—incoherent about that, too."

"Perhaps." He smiled without amusement. "But it didn't impress me. I hardly think either reckless spending or gambling are weaknesses that can be inherited. I suspect you're merely finding an easy excuse for your excesses, Miss Adams."

Pompous brute, Carrie thought. She asked him flatly, "Are you going to lend me the money, Mr. Revellion? I'll sign an IOU—give you the name of my solicitor so you can check that I'm not lying about my legacy."

"I thought you expected nothing," he said sardonically. "You're not my responsibility, you know. It might be the best thing that could happen to you to learn your lesson the hard way. Frankly, I doubt whether you'd end up in gaol, but certainly you'd have a few sleepless nights."

Carrie felt despair. She wasn't doing much to help Kim. She'd really have to snap out of it—change her tactics, and find some way of persuading him to sign that cheque.

"You expected it to be a pushover, didn't you?" he remarked after a moment. "You're a pretty girl—well, you're more than that—but unfortunately for you I'm not the usual susceptible male. In fact, I'm proof against your femininity to an extent that you wouldn't believe."

Carrie's cheeks flamed. "I don't follow you. I—I wouldn't dream of trying to appeal to you as a woman. I'm—I'm asking you the way any man would—are you going to lend me that money? Which, I repeat, I can repay almost before you've missed it."

He raised one eyebrow and his lower lip curled sensually. "Who are you trying to fool, Miss Adams? You haven't asked me the way a man would. From the moment you stepped into this room you've made me conscious of the fact that you're very feminine and very sexy. Your use of those long eyelashes—the way you blush—the graceful way you move your very alluring body. But as I've just pointed out to you, that sort of thing doesn't affect my judgement. I haven't been twisted around a female finger for a long long time."

Carrie had got to her feet, hating the fact that she was blushing again, even though it was with anger.

"You're telling me no, aren't you? Then I wish you'd just say so. You—you've got all that money and you're so high and mighty. You let me come all the way from Sydney for nothing—just to—to lecture me." She broke off, tears of anger in her eyes. What was going to happen to Kim now? What could she do? She hated Steve Revellion. He could have helped so easily, at no cost to himself. She began to think it would have been wiser for Kim to have thrown herself on his mercy—though she could see very well why she hadn't. He was so hard, so unyielding, so callous. She lowered her head and groped in her handbag for a tissue.

He had got to his feet too. "Tears," he said. "The typical resort of the human female."

Carrie wiped her tears away furiously, and as she did so she heard the sound of the front door opening, and a rather coy feminine voice called out, "Is anyone home? Are you there, Steve?"

He muttered an oath and was standing close enough to Carrie for her to hear it.

"I beg your pardon," he said. Then raising his voice, "Come in, Nella."

He needn't have bothered issuing the invitation. Already the owner of the voice, a small rather dumpy woman with a round face, round blue eyes, and wispily untidy hair that had once been red, was standing in the doorway staring at them in surprise. Carrie was suddenly conscious that she and Steve Revellion were standing rather close to each other and she moved away embarrassed, muttering, "I'd better go—" Then she caught her breath as he took hold of her arm, his fingers pressing cruelly into the flesh, so that she couldn't excape him.

The woman he'd called Nella had come right into the room, followed by a tall, svelte blonde with light blue eyes and a wide vivid mouth, her suntanned skin set off by a strapless white dress. Carrie was instantly reminded of Paul's new girlfriend, whom he'd described as tallish, blonde, elegant. This blonde was obviously older than Josie Tanner, thirty or close to it, Carrie reflected and wondered out of the blue if it was the girl who'd been mentioned obliquely in the magazine article—the girl it was rumoured Steve Revellion was about to marry. She'd meant to ask Kim about that, and had completely forgotten. She was looking at Carrie in a far from friendly way, but it was hardly Carrie's fault that Steve Revellion was hanging on to her arm the way he was. When she tried to move away, his grip grew even tighter so that she winced.

"I didn't know you had a visitor. Who's this?" the blonde exclaimed brightly and somehow patronisingly. She looked Carrie over quickly, her pale blue eyes assessing her clothes, judging them of little interest, then searching her face and noting, Carrie was certain, traces of tears. "Are we interrupting something?"

"I'm afraid you are, Janelle," Steve Revellion said. He let go of Carrie's arm and she almost jumped out of her skin as he put his arm around her waist in a decidedly familiar way. "I don't think you've met Caroline Adams, have you? Carrie— Miss Nella Higgins and Mrs. Lane—Janelle Lane."

"How do you do?" Carrie murmured, uncomfortably conscious of his hand on her hip and of the fact that Janelle Lane—*Mrs.* Lane—was aware of it too, and didn't like it one little bit. "I—I hope you'll excuse me. I was just leaving." She looked up at the man beside her and coloured deeply as she met his eyes. "I'm sorry we couldn't—sort things out better. Thank you anyhow for—" *For nothing,* she thought.

"We'll finish our talk over dinner tonight, Carrie." he said.

"What?" she exclaimed, bewildered. "But I thought you'd decided—"

"I haven't decided anything yet, Carrie." His eyes were blue and dazzling and she couldn't read the expression in them, but hope sprang to life in her. He wasn't as cold and forbidding as he had been earlier, though she couldn't imagine why he should have changed. But perhaps he'd just been tormenting her. Was there even a suspicion of a smile playing around his lips? He turned to the others to say, "I'll just see Caroline into the lift, if you'll excuse me a minute."

Miss Higgins gave Carrie a bird-like nod and then looked anxiously at Janelle Lane. Carrie murmured good-bye, and with Steve's arm still around her, was escorted from the room and into the hallway outside the flat. He pressed the button for the lift then looked at her thoughtfully, his eyes roaming over her in a leisurely way, and loitering on her breasts, her lips, her eyes.

"I presume you're staying with Kim?" She nodded. "I'll pick you up at her flat at about eight o'clock."

"Do you mean you're going to help us—me?" she stammered.

He narrowed his eyes. "We might be able to come to an arrangement of some kind. I'll think it out and we can discuss it during dinner."

Dinner! Oh heavens, he'd be sure to take her to some smart restaurant and she had nothing suitable to wear, nothing at all. She told him desperately, "I don't want to have dinner with you. I'd—I'd much rather not."

He shrugged dismissingly. "All right. Then we'll forget the whole thing, Miss Adams." The lift had come, and Carrie seized hold of his arm frantically, thinking of Kim.

"Please, I didn't mean that. I'll—I'll have dinner with you, I'll do anything you want."

"I thought you might," he said cynically. "Then I'll see you tonight, Carrie. We might be able to work out something together."

He urged her into the lift, the doors closed, and she was alone. Her heart was beating fast and she felt absolutely wrung out. What an ordeal—what an interview—what a mess! She'd really believed Kim's cause was lost and then when those two women turned up, he'd suddenly softened up. Well, you couldn't really call it softening up, she mused, and she'd have to be very careful where she put her foot tonight or he was quite likely to revert to being hostile and unhelpful. He certainly wasn't easy to get along with and even now, he'd made no promises. "We might be able to work something out together," he'd said—and she hadn't the least idea what that meant.

All the same, she felt hopeful.

Chapter Two

When she emerged from the hotel onto the Esplanade, the day had almost faded. Lights were on in the street, the sea had grown quiet, there were only a few people left on the beach. A warm wind blew in from the sea, and as she walked quickly back to Kim's flat, the scent of oleander blossoms was on the air, musky and hauntingly sweet. It was a scent that reminded her of summer nights and of Paul, and she wondered what he was doing tonight. He'd be somewhere with Josie Tanner, no doubt dining with her folks after discussing the new restaurant with her father.

Her hurt, as she thought of him, was mixed with anger and helplessness, and she pushed him fiercely to the back of her mind and began to hurry. Kim would be waiting to hear what had happened, and the news wasn't all that good. If those people—Miss

Higgins and Janelle Lane—hadn't turned up, it might have all been sorted out by now, and yet it seemed to have been their arrival that had made Steve Revellion think again about whether he'd help her out.

"What's happened?" Kim demanded a few minutes later, as she met Carrie at the door. "Did you get the cheque?"

Carrie shook her head. "I'm afraid not."

"What? But—but he's going to give it to you, isn't he?" As they spoke, the two girls moved into the living room, and Carrie sank down exhaustedly on the couch.

"I have no idea. He's picking me up here at eight tonight and we're having dinner together."

Kim was absolutely staggered. "He's taking you to dinner! Good *heavens!* But why? What's the idea?"

Carrie didn't really know. She said, "Well, these two women turned up while we were still in the midst of negotiations. Actually, it wasn't going too well because he seemed to think it would be the best thing that ever happened if I went to gaol and learned my lesson."

Kim bit her lips. "I'm sorry, Carrie. I feel really mean, because you're such a sensible sort of person. I know it's not fair, but I do have to think about my job, and then there's Gene." She frowned anxiously. "He will lend us the money, won't he? He must."

"It's no use telling me that," Carrie said. "He's not the sort of person you can wrap around your little finger. Not that I have the least idea how to wrap any man around my little finger," she added bitterly. "He doesn't like me anyhow."

"Oh, you don't have to take that personally," Kim said. "I told you he's really warped when it comes to women—all because of this girl who jilted him years ago."

"All the same, I read in an article that it's rumoured he's going to get married at last."

Kim shrugged and moved restlessly. She was more interested in her own problems than in Steve Revellion's matrimonial chances. "It may be true. I've heard he's going to marry Janelle Lane. She and her aunt are always hanging around the Gold Coast, and him, these days."

So I had been right, Carrie thought. She said aloud, "They were the people who turned up this evening—Janelle Lane and her aunt, I mean."

Kim got to her feet. "Then I wish they hadn't. I won't be able to sleep till all this business is settled, Carrie. There's so little time left and I dread having Gene find out and drop me. He'll think I'm irresponsible, and I'm not—not anymore."

Carrie sighed. "For heaven's sake, Kim, don't start crying again. I'll do my best for you, and right now I'd better find something I can wear tonight."

Kim sniffed back her tears. "I have a whole load of dinner dresses, Carrie. You're welcome to any of them."

"Then find me something with a high neck and no sexy overtones," Carrie said dryly. "Otherwise he'll think I'm trying to use my feminine wiles on him, and as likely as not that will make him decide not to lend us the money."

A few minutes later, Kim produced a fairly plain black dress.

"I never wear it now. It was always tight on me and now it's much too tight. But it won't look sexy on you," she assured Carrie. "You're too thin."

Carrie brightened it with a string of green beads,

also belonging to Kim, and wore her own plain black high-heeled sandals. She wasn't looking forward to her dinner date and the task of trying to extract from Steve Revellion, without using her femininity, the little sum of six thousand dollars. *I can't,* she thought despairingly, as she made up her face at the bathroom mirror. Kim was in the kitchen preparing a solitary meal for herself—and a fairly substantial one despite her worries. Carrie wished she could have joined her. The thought of spending maybe a couple of hours alone with that man was totally unnerving. There were things that puzzled her too, such as why he had put his arm around her when Janelle Lane was around. Kim had confirmed she was the girl he was rumoured to be marrying. Perhaps they'd had a quarrel. If that was so, then Carrie didn't like it. Nor did she like that phrase he'd used to her, about "working something out together." It made her decidedly uneasy.

From the window, she saw his car, a Mercedes, pull up outside the flats right on the dot of eight o'clock, and she snatched up the little green evening purse Kim had lent her and calling out goodbye, hurried down the stairs.

Breathless from hurrying, she almost ran into him at the outside door and he said dryly, "Don't you know it doesn't do to run to meet a man so eagerly?"

"I'm not running to meet you," she snapped back. "Or—or if I am, it's merely because I imagine you don't like to be kept waiting. It's not as if this were an ordinary sort of date."

"You're quite right, Carrie," he agreed. "It's far from being that." They crossed the narrow strip of garden, and he led her into the car. She knew he'd looked her over quickly but thoroughly when he'd encountered her, but whether he was satisfied with her appearance or not she didn't know, and she told herself she didn't care. At least she looked respectable. *It was strange,* she thought as he took the driver's seat, *to be here in a car with a man she didn't know at all—a man who was more or less a millionaire. And she was going out to dinner with him. Paul would be absolutely stunned if he knew. But, of course, he wouldn't know. Not ever.*

He said little as they drove through the brightly lit streets, crowded with tourists and holiday makers. The shops were still open, and brilliant lights illuminated discos and night clubs and restaurants. Presently Steve pulled into a parking place outside a smallish restaurant with glass walls that looked onto gardens on two sides, and onto the ocean on a third. As they went inside, she realised at once that he was well known. The maitre d' hotel greeted him by name, and showed them to a table that looked across the beach to the sea, and was partly screened by huge indoor plants whose leaves were fantastically green in the soft artificial lighting. It was incredible to Carrie that it was only last night she had dined with Paul, and he'd told her in the most casual way that they were through. Now she was having dinner on the Gold Coast with one of Australia's most eligible bachelors, and the irony of it—an irony that grew to enormous proportions as the evening advanced—was that she'd told Paul, "Maybe I'll go up to the Gold Coast and meet an elderly millionaire. Marry him." Well, she'd met a millionaire, but he wasn't elderly. Nor was she going to marry him.

Steve ordered oysters on the shell, sandcrab and salad, and white wine. The restautant was decorated with baskets of flowers and ferns, and great pots of greenery that gave it the air of a conservatory. The service was first class and so was the food, and Carrie, who had been involved in the catering business for the past three years, was impressed.

"I get the idea that despite your youthful looks you're accustomed to dining out fairly often," Steve commented presently. "Is that where some of the money goes? Or do you have a handful of escorts?"

Carrie gave him a cool smile. "I'm used to restaurant eating, yes, but I've seen most of it from the other side. I've just completed the catering supervisors certificate course."

"You surprise me," he said.

"Do I? Why?"

He shurgged. "Perhaps because it's unexpected for a girl who gets herself into such a financial muddle to be engaged in so practical a thing. Have you passed your exams?"

"Yes, every one of them," she said dryly.

"And you've started work somewhere?"

"Not actually. I've been working in a restaurant part-time, but my plans for next year have fallen through. I—I'm not sure what I'm going to do now."

He sent her a sardonic, vividly blue look. "And you're all but penniless. What a shame you've been so imprudent."

"Yes, it's a great shame," she agreed, her voice brittle. The waiter topped up her wine glass, and she asked, "Anyhow, are you going to help me out? I thought that's what we were going to discuss. I know you didn't ask me to dinner to talk about myself."

"Not altogether," he said. "But before we get down to business, I want to know a little about you. I already know your age and your propensity for throwing your money around recklessly, and I know you've completed a course in catering and that you don't have any employment at the moment." His blue eyes looked at her across the table and a little shiver ran over her skin. Anyone seeing them now would imagine they were on the closest terms, at this discreet table for two with its romantic view through waving palms and purple bougainvillea to a silvery beach and the mysterious dark of the ocean. And now he leaned across and looked into her eyes in the candlelight. "How about boyfriends, Carrie? Is there anyone special?"

Carrie's eyes fell before the intensity of his regard. She felt the deepest reluctance to mention Paul, and after all, why should she? It was nothing to do with him whether she had a boyfriend or not, and certainly none of his business that she'd just been dropped. She said coolly, "No, there's no one special. I've been too busy the last three years for—for that kind of thing."

"Well, if you say so," he said after a moment. "But I find it hard to believe. You're very attractive as you doubtless know, and you appear to be fairly intelligent—except when it comes to money."

Carrie pressed her lips together and said nothing. The waiter smoothly removed their entree plates, the wine waiter poured them a little more wine, and Steve Revellion said in a businesslike way, "Now, about family. What do you have in the way of relatives? I gather you're either short of them or else not on good terms. Otherwise you wouldn't have had to burden Kim with your troubles."

Carrie sipped her wine. She hadn't burdened Kim with her troubles, and it was maddening to be unable to say so. She told him, "My parents are dead, and I have no brothers and sisters. I do have relatives in

England, but I don't know them. I was born in Dorset, but my father died when I was very small and my mother decided to come back home to Australia."

Their main course arrived, and Carrie stopped talking and stole a look at him. She was positive he didn't want to hear all the details of her life history. It could have nothing whatever to do with whether or not he was going to make her a loan. She suspected he was merely prolonging the agony, making her sing for her supper, as it were. She went on determinedly, "My mother had two sisters in Sydney—my Aunt Janet, who's Kim's mother, and Aunt Lena—the one who left me the legacy." She raised her eyes to see if he believed that.

"Ah, yes, the famous legacy," he said, his mouth curving in a cynical smile. "Are you going to help yourself to salad or do you prefer to have it later?"

"I'll have it later, thank you. This crab is really delicious."

"I agree. But let's get back to your saga."

She gave him a quizzical look. "Must we? I can't imagine it's of any interest to you. . . . Well, my mother contracted a serious illness soon after we came to Sydney, and had to go to the hospital, so Kim's parents looked after me, and when my mother died, I stayed on with them. Kim and I were brought up more or less as sisters."

"How old were you then, Caroline?"

"Just old enough to go off to school with Kim, fortunately. She was six and I was five. Aunt Janet worked, you see, and couldn't have stayed home to look after me."

"So who did you inherit your gambling instincts

from?" he asked unexpectedly. "Was it your father?"

She blushed scarlet with shock. It went against the grain to say that her father had been a gambler. She couldn't do it.

"It was—it was someone further back in the family, I think," she said wildly, and he regarded her cynically.

"Are you sure it's not just something you invented to excuse your weakness?"

"Quite sure," she said evenly, and that was true enough. "What else do you want to know about me, Mr. Revellion?" she asked with a forced smile.

"Just one thing," he said. "Do you expect me to make you this loan for nothing? Or do you realise that one usually has to pay for what one receives?"

"What do you mean?" she asked warily. "Do you—do you mean you'd expect me to pay interest?" Their glances met across the table and her heart began to pound suddenly. She was quite sure he hadn't meant that, and the thought came unbidden into her head that he was going to ask her to sleep with him. At once she rejected that and wanted to laugh hysterically. The look in his eyes didn't mean that. Besides, a man like Steve Revellion wouldn't stoop to exacting such a payment. All the same her throat was dry, and she reached for her glass with a hand that shook.

"No, I don't mean that," he said, his glance not leaving her face. "I'm not interested in extracting money from you. But if I help you, then you must earn my help."

Carrie fiddled with her wine glass. She wished she hadn't thought along such idiotic lines. She stammered out, "Well, yes, of course. I—I could work in the hotel. I'm—I'm quite capable as a waitress or—or I could help with the cost control or something. I'll—I'll do anything you say."

"Will you? That's rather a rash statement. In any event, I'm not looking for an unpaid employee. You'd be a lot more use to me in a quite different capacity, Carrie."

"What do you want of me?" she asked.

He didn't answer straight away and she looked at him warily, taking in anew the thick curling black hair, the lean brown cheeks, the jewel blue eyes. He was disturbingly good to look at, yet despite the romantic candlelight of the restaurant, she had no illusions about him. He was hard and calculating. She could see it in those unreadable, enigmatic eyes, in the tough line of his jaw. What on earth was he going to ask her to do? *I wouldn't trust him an inch,* she told herself. In fact, after Paul's letting her down as he had, she didn't think she'd ever trust a man again. They thought of themselves first, last and always.

Her dinner temporarily forgotten, she bit nervously on her lower lip, waiting for him to speak, certain he was going to ask something outrageous though she couldn't for the life of her think what it could be. He'd warned her you can't expect anything for nothing, and for sure *he* hadn't got where he was by being soft and kind-hearted and generous. Yet how on earth could *she* be any use to him?

Her wine glass had been unobtrusively filled again and she reached for it and sipped some of the cool dryish wine.

"I want you to marry me, Caroline," he said, looking straight and unsmilingly into her eyes.

"What?" Carrie nearly choked. She set down her glass with a sharp little thud. She'd had too much to drink. She was hearing things—she must be. He couldn't possibly have said what she thought he'd said. "Marry you?" she repeated shakily. "You—you're joking! Besides you—you're going to marry that girl I met this afternoon—Janelle Lane."

His eyebrows peaked and one corner of his long mouth lifted sardonically. "So you've heard that rumour already, have you? From Kim, I suppose. Well, I'm not marrying Janelle. If I were I'd hardly be suggesting what I am. And I assure you I'm not joking, I'm perfectly serious."

Carrie had the feeling that in a moment she was going to pass out cold. She was going right off her head. Marry him!—when they'd only met this afternoon, and it hadn't been exactly a friendly meeting at that.

"Are you going to have some of this salad?" she heard him ask.

"No—yes." Carrie felt so dizzy and confused she hardly knew what she was saying. She helped herself to salad, not at all sure that she was going to be capable of doing more than push it around the plate. "I just don't get it," she murmured. "Why should you ask me to—to—" She stopped, incapable of going on, and he finished for her.

"Marry me?"

She met his eyes briefly and lowered her own. "Yes. We don't know the first thing about each other."

"I don't entirely agree with you," he said smoothly. "You've told me something about yourself tonight, and I daresay you've heard one or two things about me quite apart from the odd rumour."

"*One* rumour," she insisted contrarily. "And–and after all, Mrs. Lane *is* staying in your apartment, isn't she?"

His mouth set in a hard line. "She *and* her aunt," he corrected her, and went on unsmilingly, "You're like all women, aren't you—young as you are? Too curious for your own good. You want to know all about things that don't concern you."

Her lashes flew up. "Honestly, Mr. Revellion! Things that don't concern me! You ask me to marry you—and then you're surprised because I ask questions. Am I expected to be so over-awed, so flattered, that I just spring to attention and say, 'Yes, Mr. Revellion, certainly, Mr. Revellion. When am I to present myself at the—the church, Mr. Revellion?'"

His nostrils dilated slightly and he permitted himself a grim smile but he didn't apologise. He said, "In your position, with an offer like I've made you, I wouldn't have expected you to be worrying about rumours."

"In *my* position?" Carrie, who had taken another mouthful of wine, said it indignantly. "What on earth are you talking about?"

He looked at her cynically. "I had the impression your position was desperate. That's how Kim described it."

With an effort she reminded herself of why she was here. Somehow, his extraordinary proposition had practically driven it from her mind. She fiddled with her glass, feeling somewhat subdued.

"Yes, well, of course we—I—do want that loan. Very badly. But it's just for a few weeks—just till I can pay you back, that's all. So you can't really expect me to—to rush into something so permanent, with my eyes shut. I'm not as desperate as *that.*"

"No? I thought you were so scared at the prospect of a term in prison—or even a night—that you'd do anything. . . . But I haven't yet explained that if you agree to my proposition, then of course, your debt to me would be forgotten. As my wife—" He paused while the waiter removed their dishes and Carrie stared at him dizzily. His wife! Suddenly the full force of it all hit her. Steve Revellion had asked her, Carrie Adams, to marry him. Could he possibly have fallen in love with her? Was that why he'd asked her? For a wild moment her eyes were fixed on him as though she were mesmerised—imagining his mouth pressed passionately against her own, his arms holding her body close against his— Not the way it had been with Paul, who'd kissed her and then let her go. He—Steve—wouldn't let her go until—

She moved her head sharply as if to clear it. She had only to say yes, and Kim would be out of her financial mess. And Aunt Lena's legacy would be intact. And she, Carrie Adams, would be bound to a stranger, sleeping in his bed, bearing his children. She looked at him wide eyed, unable to imagine it.

"Carrie," he said. "I asked you if you want dessert."

She shook her head, unable to find her voice, heard him say something to the waiter who presently moved away. Then, when his attention returned to her, she asked flatly, as though she'd planned it, which she hadn't, "I really must know why you're asking this of me, Mr. Revellion."

"For heavens sake, call me Steve," he said with faint irritability. He stared at her hard for fully a minute, his eyes narrowed in thought. "Well, if you must have a reason, I'll give you one. But don't expect it to be in the least romantic. You're undoubtedly a very fetching girl, but I'm afraid I haven't fallen madly in love with you."

She blushed deeply, embarrassed because of what she'd been thinking only a minute ago. "Oh, I know it's not that," she said brightly. "I can't say I've exactly fallen in love with you, either."

That left him totally unmoved. He shifted his elbow as the waiter placed on the table two small cups of black coffee, two tiny crystal glasses containing a liqueur of some kind, and a silver dish of homemade sweets, each in its own tiny paper lace doily.

"To come to my reason," he said then. "In a few words—I want a wife. And since I gave up long ago looking at women through a rosy mist"—he paused, his lips twisting—"forgive me if I'm too blunt but—as I see it, one woman will do as well as another." He bent his head to stir sugar into his coffee, then looked up at her again. "Within certain personal limits, of course," he added.

The blankness, the impersonality of those amazingly blue eyes rocked Carrie. It was incredible that a man could ask you to marry him and then say what he had just said, in the way he'd said it. She was both affronted and shocked. Too blunt? Of course he was too blunt. Sophisticated as he was, he could easily have put his case more tactfully if he'd chosen to do so. But he obviously didn't care about her feelings. She drank some coffee, sipped her liqueur, diagnosed it with some part of her mind as being Van der Hum, from the tangerine flavour. Her cheeks were still flushed and she was suddenly conscious that more than one person in the restaurant was interested in her—because she was with Steve Revellion. They'd be even more interested if they knew he'd just asked her to marry him—*and how,* she thought, wryly. With the uncompromising addendum that one woman will do as well as another. So flattering! That brought her back to Janelle Lane, and she said a little confusedly, "Then in that case, why aren't you marrying Janelle Lane? Rumours don't start from nothing."

His brows came together in a frown of annoyance. "If you must have it, then yes, I had thought of marrying her. But I've told you I'm not doing so, and surely that's all you need to know."

"Yes, but—she's staying in your apartment," she floundered.

He tapped angrily on the table with his knuckles. "She *and her aunt* are staying in my apartment," he said, as he had said before. "It's a privilege they had while my father was alive, and I see no reason to be churlish and put an end to it. For your further information, Max Lane—Janelle's husband—was a close friend of my father's, and almost of his generation. He managed my father's cattle station on the Darling Downs for years, right up until the day he was killed in a small plane crash about a year and a half ago. Janelle and her aunt still live on the property. My father regarded them as part of the family."

Carrie was slightly nonplussed. She'd had no idea there were ties like that. "Your father," she said hesitantly. "Did he live on the cattle station, too?"

"He spent the greater part of the last two years of his life there, and Janelle and Nella were good to him. He'd been a sick man for some time, which is why I'd taken over for him at Revellion-West. He died seven months ago. And that, I think, is all you need to know of my personal affairs for the time being."

Was it? Carrie was far from sure. It seemed to her, perhaps mistakenly, that if you were considering marrying a man, then you had a right to know a lot more than that about him. But, of course, she wasn't thinking of marrying him. She felt very confused and she knew she shouldn't have drunk that liqueur. She took a candy from the silver dish, hoping rather foolishly that it might clear her head. She nibbled at the sweet, and looked across at him, her dark eyes puzzled. "I'm sorry, but I still don't understand. I mean—why me? There must be lots of other girls who—who know you a whole lot better."

"Oh for heaven's sake," he said impatiently. "Must we go over and over it? I'm well aware that I'm regarded as a good catch, and that there are half a dozen women angling for me, but frankly I don't fancy being caught. And I don't like being manipulated. Look at it this way, you've turned up at a strategic moment, a girl who's easy on the eye, has an agreeable voice, and is definitely nubile. And if a little flattery will help things along, I'll admit I've never seen such eyes," he continued almost sardonically. "They're not black after all, I've discovered. Rather treacle coloured. Give me a little more time and I might come up with a more pleasing comparison."

"Please don't bother," Carrie said, faintly nettled. She tried desperately to sort out what she wanted to say. "You're trying to—to pressure me into this, but you're only thinking of what *you* want. What about me? Why ever should I agree to marry you?"

His brows rose. "Are you *serious?* I really shouldn't have let you drink all that wine. Surely you can't be so dumb as to believe all the benefits go to me. There are quite a few in it for you—to begin with, and this is pretty basic, you're in a spot and I'm willing to help you out on very generous terms. Secondly, I doubt whether many proposals of marriage will come your way. You're definitely a bad bet with your little habit of overspending. My guess is that's the reason you don't have a boyfriend—they've all been frightened off." Carrie tried to protest, but he went on regardless. "Finally—and maybe I should have put this at the top of the list—as my wife, you'll have absolutely everything that women seem to want."

"Except—" Carrie began and stopped. Except love, was what she'd meant to say, but somehow she couldn't bring herself to say it. It was too personal. And then, before he could ask her any questions, she said rapidly, "All the same, I couldn't possibly marry you, Mr. Revellion. I'd much sooner we just had a business arrangement."

His blue eyes hardened. "Haven't I made myself clear? As far as I'm concerned, Miss Adams, this *is* a business arrangement. I've stated my terms, and you can accept them or not, as you please. Yours is the choice. If you don't accept, then as far as I'm concerned, that's the end of it. You can make other arrangements with someone else. Your problems aren't of my making, you know."

Carrie stared at him disbelievingly. He meant she had to marry him to get that loan for Kim. And then, of course, it wouldn't be a loan—she wouldn't have to pay the money back. She'd be his wife. It wasn't fair. She couldn't possibly marry him. Surely he must see that, no matter what benefits were in it for her. She couldn't *marry* . . . a stranger—

She looked across at him and shook her head helplessly.

"I . . . couldn't."

His lip curled. "Very well. Have you finished your coffee?"

"Yes, thank you."

He pushed back his chair. "Then I'll see you home."

Carrie stood up, unable to believe it. That was it. He wasn't going to help her. She felt she hated him. He was so hard, so heartless.

Chapter Three

In a very few minutes she was sitting beside him in his car and they were driving back to Kim's.

Carrie looked out at the darkness of the sea, and the long white lines of foam where the breakers curled quietly in. The night was warm, there were people walking along the Esplanade, groups still gathered on the sand. Leaning back on the comfortable seat, Carrie knew that she was at least a little drunk, and she began to think of Kim, who'd be waiting for her to come in, flourishing a cheque, triumphant. It had seemed so certain he'd make the loan, because Carrie could pay it back so quickly. What on earth were they going to do now, with only five days left before the finance company took action? Carrie could imagine Kim's tears, her despair. And meanwhile, that hateful, callous man sat behind the steering wheel completely ignoring her. Her problems were not of his making, and he didn't care what became of her. He was probably thinking right now that it would serve her right if she were sent to gaol.

Was he thinking that? She glanced at him and found he was looking straight ahead of him. He had a handsome profile, a straight nose, a strong chin. The black curling hair gave him a wildly romantic look that was totally deceptive. He was long past being romantic! One woman was as good as another. . . . *And perhaps one man was as good—or as bad—as another,* she thought tiredly, her mind going momentarily to Paul. In fact—why not say yes after all? She moved a little in her seat. Not every girl got the chance to marry a man of his standing, and apart from everything else, it would solve a whole lot of problems. And wouldn't it be a surprise for Paul!— especially on top of her flippant remarks about millionaires.

She straightened up and looked at the man beside her. "Mr. Revellion, I—I think I've changed my mind," she said recklessly.

"You think so, do you?" He didn't sound particularly interested. He didn't brake or even look at her. He simply drove on.

Here we go, she thought. *Sing for your supper.*

She said, "Yes. Well, I know I have. So can we talk about it again—please?"

He slowed down and pulled up, and switched off the engine. Carrie could hear the subdued roar of the sea as it surged ceaselessly in to the shore. He turned towards her and put his arm along the back of the seat behind her head. His face was close to hers and she could see the glitter of his blue eyes, and she imagined she could feel the warmth of his breath.

"I thought you'd come to your senses," he said. "You'd have to be a very unusual girl to say no and mean it, under the circumstances. As a gambling girl, you should wake up to the fact you've won the jackpot this time, and you'd be a fool to walk off without collecting it."

Carrie swallowed. She was suddenly and frighteningly aware of his closeness, and her heart began to beat so fast she could feel it throbbing against her rib cage. She said stutteringly, drawing back from him slightly, "If—if you mean you're such a great prize, I—I don't agree."

"Oh, I don't mean myself personally, Carrie," he said mockingly. "I mean what my money can give you."

She struggled with an idea that was forming in her mind. After all, he'd talked about business deals, so—"Do you mean it won't be a—real marriage?" she forced herself to ask. "You won't expect me to—"

"I'll expect you to sleep with me, if that's what you want to know. Or do you think I look like a man who's satisfied with a figurehead of a wife?"

"I—I don't know," she mumbled.

"Then perhaps I should demonstrate to you that I'm made of real flesh and blood," he said, and before she knew what was happening she was in his arms, her mouth crushed against his in a kiss that set out deliberately to stir her senses. She knew from her small experience with Paul that kissing could provoke all kinds of reactions, but Paul's kisses had been nothing like this. Steve's hand was against her breast and she felt the delicate but assured movement of his fingers as they stroked her nipple, and even through Kim's dress, and her thin bra, it was infinitely disturbing.

She'd been so completely taken by surprise she hadn't had a chance to resist, and now she was in a helpless position, pressed back against the seat, his body half-covering hers. Her senses were in such a turmoil she discovered she was actually clinging to him, reaching one hand to the back of his head where she could feel the crisp curling of his dark hair.

She was on the point of struggling when he let her go, and said abstractedly, "I've admitted I'm not a romantic, but making love in the front seat of a car really doesn't appeal to me. Something will have to be done about it."

Carrie's heart was pounding hard, and everything seemed so unreal that she knew quite certainly she'd taken too much alcohol. Otherwise, she would never have let this happen. Then, suddenly, she remembered why she'd let it happen, and she said with an odd clarity, "You'll write out that cheque for me, won't you?"

She heard him utter a brief exclamation. "You mercenary little female! Surely you don't expect me to write out a cheque in the middle of making love to you!"

"But you've stopped now," she said ridiculously. She raised a hand to smooth back her hair and gasped with shock as he gripped her wrist and pulled her hand down to rest on the hardness of his thigh.

"I'm tempted to go on—right here in this car seat," he said harshly, then to her relief he released her abruptly, moved away from her and started up the car again. "Is Kim home tonight?"

"Yes," she said huskily. "You—you can't come up to the flat."

"Then that's lucky for you." He was driving fast and she knew he was angry with her, though surely she couldn't have hurt his feelings—because she was quite sure she meant nothing to him. He wanted a wife, and for some reason she couldn't fathom, it was to be her. *Surely Janelle Lane hadn't refused him,* she thought bewilderedly, and he had chosen this way to save his face. It would explain his extraordinary proposal to a certain degree but—no, she couldn't believe that Janelle Lane wouldn't positively leap at the chance of marrying him. She had been convinced by now that he would make their marriage a real one, and one part of her was so alarmed she wanted to call it off—tell him she'd changed her mind again. Yet with another part of her mind she half-expected him to forestall her—to tell her his proposition was withdrawn, because he didn't want a wife who talked about money in the middle of his lovemaking. And then what were she and Kim going to do? Carrie didn't know if she wanted to laugh hysterically or if she wanted to weep. Most of all, perhaps, she wanted to wake up and find it had all been no more than a freaky dream.

There was a light shining from Kim's flat when he pulled up outside, and getting out of the car he walked round to open the door for her. He said nothing and Carrie wanted to ask about the cheque but couldn't make herself say the words. After a moment, she said in a low voice, "Thank you for the dinner, Mr. Revellion." Oh, heavens—how absurd it sounded! She looked up at him and found he was staring down at her.

"I'll see you tomorrow, Carrie. I have some business matters to attend to first, so we'll make it twelve o'clock. I'll pick you up here and we can have some lunch and discuss our coming relationship."

And the cheque, the cheque, she repeated feverishly over and over in her head, willing him to mention it because she couldn't. She realised hazily that she should tell him the name of the finance company, but she couldn't remember it. Or–or had she told him already? She couldn't remember that, either. In fact, she was in a mental turmoil.

"You'd better go in and get some sleep," he told her. "And next time I take you out, don't drink so much wine if you don't have the head for it. With your training, you should know better. Do you want me to see you up the stairs?"

"No, of course not," she exclaimed, hating that he thought she'd drunk too much, even though she had. "I'm perfectly all right. I'm just—just tired. I haven't drunk too much." The palms in the little garden rattled in the warm night wind, and she looked up at him seeing him clearly in the lights from the flat—that thick curling hair that she'd actually run her fingers through. She shivered at the memory, and saw one corner of his mouth lift in a brief smile.

"Good night, Carrie."

"Good night, Mr. Revellion."

"Steve," he said. "Get used to it. You're going to marry me soon."

She swallowed. "Yes. Good night—Steve." She turned away and went rapidly to the entrance door then had to fumble in her purse for the key Kim had given her. *Soon,* he'd said. *How soon?* As she went upstairs, she began to wonder what she'd done. Agreeing to that preposterous proposal! She must have been clean out of her mind. She should have let him drive her straight home after she'd said no, instead of panicking and changing her mind. Kim would never in a fit expect *this* of her, no matter what happened. She half-turned, ready to run down the stairs and tell him she'd changed her mind. But he'd driven off by now—and she could tell him tomorrow. It wouldn't make any difference.

In the living room, Kim jumped up from the sofa where she was sprawling to ask, "Is it all fixed? What's happened?"

Carrie discovered that the light made her feel dizzy and just a little sick, and she sank down in a chair. How on earth was she going to tell Kim what had happened? She just wasn't going to believe it.

Kim was leaning down and shaking her by the shoulder. "Carrie—what's up? What *has* happened?"

Carrie said weakly, "He wants to marry me."

Kim stared at her and frowned. *"Carrie!* You don't know what you're saying! *Who* wants to marry you? What on earth are you talking about?"

Carrie drew a deep breath. "Steve Revellion. I—I know I've had a little too much to drink, Kim, but it's true."

Kim looked frankly skeptical. "Okay, if you say so. But what about the money, Carrie? Did you get the cheque?"

Carrie shook her head. "Not yet. I'm sorry—"

"Not yet!" Kim dropped down on the floor with a little groan. "But, Carrie, that was the whole *point* of it all. And then you come home like—like this and talk about marrying him."

"But he did—" Carrie began, and Kim broke in almost angrily.

"Oh, don't say it again, Carrie. He's going to marry Janelle Lane. His aunt practically told me so, and I know it's true."

"Well, it's not true," Carrie said. "I asked him and he said he wasn't, and if you'll just give me a chance to explain—" She stopped and took a deep breath. "He won't lend us the money unless I agree to marry him, and you can make all the faces you like, Kim, but that's exactly what he said."

Kim looked utterly flabbergasted. Finally she said weakly, "But didn't you tell him you could pay it all back in a few weeks?"

"Yes, I did, and he's not interested. Either I agree, or we get nothing." She waited for Kim to protest that it was ridiculous, and that of course she wouldn't hear of Carrie doing anything so crazy, that they'd manage somehow.

Instead, her cousin said slowly, "It's like something out of a TV film. Steve Revellion wants you to marry him! Oh, Carrie, you're so lucky! You'd have to be mad to say no." She opened her blue eyes wide. "You did say yes, didn't you? I would have, like a shot."

Carrie leaned back wearily. "I said yes—but I wish I hadn't. And now if you don't mind, I'm going to bed. I've got an absolutely splitting headache."

When she woke in the morning it was to find Kim already dressed and making up her rather plump little face at the bedroom mirror.

"Hi!" She looked at Carrie through the glass. "Did you sleep well?"

Carrie had slept like a log, but now she sat up, remembering, and felt sick. *She'd actually agreed to marry Steve Revellion.* Kim was looking at her curiously, and now she turned round and came to stand beside the bed.

"Do you remember what you told me last night, Carrie?" she asked anxiously. "Or have you forgotten?"

Carrie sighed. "I haven't forgotten—no such luck. But I can't possibly go through with it, Kim. You told me I'd be mad to say no, but I was madder still to say yes. I'm seeing him today—I'll tell him it's all off."

"Don't be stupid!" Kim exclaimed. "Just think of it—you'll have everything you want for the rest of your life. No dragging yourself off to work every day—you won't even have to slog away cleaning your house and getting meals for the family, and all that sort of thing. I only wish I had the chance. You wouldn't catch *me* turning it down."

"Then perhaps it's a shame you didn't tell the truth," Carrie said shortly. "He might have proposed to you then, instead of to me."

"I don't think so," was Kim's retort. "He's never taken any notice of me at all, except to stop by once in a blue moon and ask if I'm happy with the conditions at the Daystar. There must be something about you that really attracts him, that's for sure."

Carrie slid out of bed and wandered across to the window. She knew there was nothing about her that attracted Steve Revellion. He'd said he liked her eyes, but he'd also said that one woman would do as well as another—which was hardly flattering. What a basis for a marriage! When she thought what she'd done, she felt sick in the pit of her stomach. She remembered him kissing her in the car down by the beach, and how she'd mentioned that cheque, and she felt she'd die if she had to even see him again.

"You'll have to get rid of that old nightgown before you marry him," Kim said. "It looks like something left over from boarding school—not a bit sexy!"

Carrie turned away from the window and the already brilliant sunshine.

"I *am* going to call it off, Kim," she said sombrely. "I didn't know what I was doing last night. It was the wine—the liqueur. We'll borrow the money from somebody else."

Kim's face grew stormy. "There *isn't* anybody else, Carrie," she exclaimed, her lower lip trembling childishly. "Do you think I haven't racked my brains night after night trying to think who I could turn to? And now—just when everything's working out so marvellously—and we wouldn't even have to pay the money back—you tell me it's all off. It's not fair." A couple of tears rolled down her cheeks and before Carrie could think what to say, she suddenly brightened up. "Carrie! Oh, of course! Look—why don't you just get engaged to him—get the cheque—and then, when Aunt Lena's money arrives, tell him you've changed your mind? It wouldn't hurt you to go along with him for a few weeks, would it?"

Wouldn't it? With a man like Steve Revellion, Carrie was far from sure about that. She said reluctantly, "But it wouldn't be honest, would it?"

"Oh, don't be silly! You'd pay the money back. That's not being dishonest. Besides, by then, you might have changed your mind about breaking it off."

"And I might not have," Carrie said. "Well, I'll think about it while I have my shower."

It was all so easy for Kim, looking at it from the outside, she thought a few minutes later, as she stripped off the nightgown that looked like something left over from boarding school, and stepped under the shower. But it mightn't be all that easy to stall off her marriage for five weeks or so. Steve would probably want to make love to her anyhow, and the strain of keeping that under control would be really something. He'd demonstrated his virility and his male strength very ably in the car last night.

Kim came to the door to say that she was leaving for work.

"You won't call it all off, will you Carrie? Please—it will ruin my life."

And what about my *life?* Carrie wondered as she answered with a sigh, "Don't worry, Kim. I'll get that money for you somehow—I'll think of a way."

But how? she asked herself in the bedroom, as she dressed in white shorts and a lilac and white striped top. There was only one way, and that was through Steve Revellion, who was callous enough to take advantage of her predicament. It would really serve him right if she reneged at the last moment, and simply paid back the money and vanished. If he wanted a wife so badly he'd have no trouble finding another girl to take her place. And his opinion of women was apparently already so low that to be jilted again wasn't going to make much difference.

Brushing her hair at the mirror, she stared frowningly at her reflection. It was really incomprehensible that he'd chosen her. She thought of Janelle Lane, tall, elegant, blonde. The kind of girl that men preferred. The kind of girl Paul apparently preferred, from his brief description of Josie Tanner. Carried looked at herself critically—her slight figure, her small firm breasts, her unremarkable face. Her eyes were her best feature—dark and shining, thickly lashed. Treacle coloured, he'd said. As she laid down her brush she noticed with a guilty shock the dark bruise on her wrist. That was where he'd grabbed her last night when she'd angered him. What a hateful, arrogant, domineering male he was! He thought he merely had to issue a command and it would be obeyed. Well, he'd find out. . . . She was glad she'd flicked him on the raw over his lovemaking last night. And on consideration, she knew she was going to do as Kim had suggested—go along with his outrageous proposal, then break it off when she got her money. The tricky thing would be to put off the marriage. After all, he'd said *"soon."* She'd have to say she wanted to get to know him better, or something like that. Nothing about the manoeuvre appealed to her, because ordinarily she was a girl who kept her promises and meant what she said. Well, she had firsthand knowledge that men weren't so scrupulous. Paul hadn't hesitated to put himself first, and that was what she must learn to do. It was the only way once you were out in the world.

She combed her hair to one side, twisted it deftly and tied it with a lilac ribbon. When she'd tidied the bedroom, she made herself coffee and toast, and after she'd breakfasted and washed up, she decided to walk down to the beach. She decided not to swim. She'd have to be back in time to change and be ready for Steve, and she didn't want to spend time washing the salt out of her hair.

It was only a couple of minutes walk to the beach—a long area of shining white sand that stretched out as far as one could see in either direction. All winter, people came up from the southern states to enjoy the sunshine here and in summer they came from the inland, too. High-rise hotels and motels and apartment blocks had not yet entirely taken over, but much of the natural beauty of the coast—the scrub, the tea trees, the dunes— had disappeared. Carrie thought inevitably of the magazine article, and how Steve Revellion had said his company wouldn't be putting up any more high-rise buildings on the land it had acquired. It was a little heartening to find she could approve of something he had done. . . .

She made her way onto the beach by a narrow path cut through sand that was covered with coarse grass—grass that was being carefully nurtured since big storms had washed away beaches no longer protected by dunes and natural vegetation. On the beach, everyone was either soaking up the sun, braving the surf between the safety flags, or, further along, riding surfboards. It wasn't as fashionable here as the part of the beach opposite Cavill Avenue, but all the same it was fairly crowded, and Carrie, flinging herself down on the sand, face down, amused herself watching the crowd, and deliberately avoided thinking of what was ahead of her.

She sat up abruptly when a tall bosomy girl in a tiny blue bikini walked up towards her from the surf. Carrie recognised her instantly as Janelle Lane. She looked like a goddess, her tanned body glistening, her blonde hair sleeked back and dark with water. Carrie saw several males eyeing her as she strolled up the beach with all the self-possession that the consciousness of beauty gave, checking the long blue earrings that dangled from her ears. She'd be furious when she discovered that Carrie was engaged to Steve Revellion. There was nothing surer, and Carrie watched her nervously as she came closer. All the same, she was prepared to smile, and it was a shock when the other girl gave her a haughty glance and walked straight past her. Carrie drew a sharp breath. Was that deliberate? She turned, and found Janelle was looking back at her. Carrie removed her sunglasses and smiled. There was no response and she blushed to the roots of her hair. It wasn't amusing to be cut dead, and she felt shaken and upset. Obviously, the other girl disliked her already. Had Steve told her of his plans to marry Caroline?

She didn't stay on the beach much longer, the pleasure had gone out of it, and she reflected as she walked back to the Esplanade that it wasn't going to be much fun being engaged to Steve Revellion. It was no use hoping she wouldn't have to meet Janelle Lane again, she was sure she would, and her feeling of distaste for the whole thing increased as she walked slowly back to the flat.

She had half an hour to fill in, and as she walked past the shop she toyed with the idea of buying something new—something stunning—to wear to lunch today. But, after all, she didn't want to fascinate Steve Revellion, so why bother? Why waste her money? At the flat, she poured herself a cold drink and switched on the radio. It didn't stop her thinking of him all the time, and it began to annoy her that her whole mind was so completely taken over by the man. Still, at least it had stopped her brooding over Paul, if that was any comfort. She'd started towards the bedroom with the intention of changing out of her shorts when the doorbell rang. Her heart began to pound and her pulses raced as she went to the door.

It was Steve, of course, in tobacco brown shirt and off-white pants. Carrie was instantly aware of her own careless appearance, the ridiculous twist of hair caught at the side of her neck, the wind-blown tendrils that drifted across her forehead. She was conscious too that those brilliantly blue eyes of his were sweeping over her in a critical fashion that made her aware of every part of her body, particularly of her legs, so well revealed by the crumpled shorts.

"Oh, it's you," she exclaimed, feigning negligence. "Will you come in? I'm not quite ready."

His mouth curved in a sardonic smile. "I can see that." He came in and closed the door behind him, then walked past her into the living room, where he stood looking around at Kim's expensive and slightly garish furnishings, and the profusion of pictures and ornaments she'd collected. He strolled across to a cabinet to pick up a Balinese carving of a graceful and obviously male figure, with head tilted back and hands pressed together in the shape of a flame.

"You cousin has—expensive tastes," he commented as he set it down again.

He was right, and Carrie wondered if he'd draw any conclusions from the fact that one of his junior employees could indulge such whims. She said wildly, "Some of these things are—are gifts."

"Really?"

"Yes. From Aunt Lena and—" She broke off. It would be indiscreet to name Gene Lennox, and of course she was pretty sure that Kim had bought all this stuff herself on various shopping sprees—the *mille fleur* paper weight, the little silver pig that was a mustard pot, the miniature chandelier that hung rather ostentatiously from the ceiling. "I'd better get dressed," she said. "If you'll excuse me. Please sit down."

He didn't accept her invitation. Instead he moved towards her purposefully. "Aren't you forgetting something, Carrie?"

"What?" she breathed, colour suffusing her cheeks as she found herself trapped in his quizzical blue stare. She was sure she knew what he meant, of course—she knew from the way his eyes travelled to her mouth, to her breasts, then back to her eyes. He meant she should greet him with a kiss. Her tongue came out to moisten her upper lip and she raised her face a little, her eyes half-closed.

For several seconds nothing happened, and then he said mockingly, "You've forgotten to ask if I've brought your cheque."

Carrie's eyes flew open and she stared at him furiously. He was looking amused, and he knew perfectly well she'd mistaken his meaning. He'd probably done it deliberately, to pay her out for last night. She turned her face away from his cynicism. "I know you can't have brought it. I—I didn't tell you who to make it out to."

"You told me that within the first five minutes of our meeting," he retorted. "I'm accustomed to remembering such details. However, to relieve your mind, the cheque's here in my pocket, and I'll give it to you in just a minute."

She waited resignedly. Now he'd outline the conditions under which she was to receive it—ask again for her promise that she'd marry him, and she would have to lie and give it.

Instead, he put one hand on her bare upper arm, and with the fingers of his other hand he pulled undone the ribbon that was tied just below her ear. Deliberately he loosened her hair, tangling his fingers in it, and then he kissed her. Away from the confines of the car, she soon discovered a kiss had completely new meanings, new dimensions. One hand still twisted in her hair, the other explored the skin under her striped top. He unclipped her bra and his fingers found her bare breasts. She moved her mouth jerkily from his to breathe out, "Is—is this in the contract, Mr. Revellion?"

"Everything's in the contract, Miss Adams—everything," he said, his lips touching hers again so delicately she shivered at the exquisite sensation it generated. "We're going to be married, remember?"

She felt goose pimples on her skin, felt her nipples stiffen. His thighs were hard against her legs as he put his mouth to hers and parted her lips. She'd never been kissed like this before. Paul had never dared—perhaps never wanted—to go so far. Carrie had never been so roused, so much aware of her own body—and of the man's who was holding her. When he'd finished kissing her his lips slid to her neck, just below her ear, and at the exact moment when his teasing became unbearable and she knew that she wanted—must have, she didn't know what, but something more, much more—he let her go.

He loosened her fingers that were clinging to him, feeling the warmth of muscularity of his back through the silk shirt. "Go and get dressed, Carrie." He straightened her shirt with one hand and while his eyes searched hers probingly, he reached into his pocket and produced an envelope. "Here's your cheque. You know what it's for, don't you?"

Instantly, shamingly, she felt as if he were paying

her for—for letting him touch her the way he had. And for . . . future favours. She said tremulously, "What do you mean?"

"You realise exactly what I expect you to give me in exchange for this?" He still held the envelope between his fingers.

Carrie bit her lip. Her whole body was still in confusion and she wanted to be back in his arms, her body close to his. She despised herself utterly for it. He was a stranger, to whom she meant nothing. She didn't know what was happening to her life. It had turned completely upside down. She swayed slightly and he put out a hand to steady her.

"You're giving me your promise that you'll be my wife, my lover, the mother of my children."

She felt the blood go from her face and her throat was so dry she couldn't answer him. She didn't mean to marry him, and yet just now, in his arms, she'd lost her head completely.

"Well?" He tilted her face up to his, two fingers under her chin, so that she was forced to meet his eyes. "Say it," he insisted. "Give me your promise."

"What if I—won't?" she faltered.

His mouth twisted. "Then you don't get this."

Five seconds passed.

"I—I give you my promise," she said, her voice low.

"Good. I thought you'd be sensible. Then go and get dressed."

She went, her legs shaking. In the bedroom, she sank down on the bed and stared at the envelope. Inside it was a cheque for six thousand dollars. She thought of Kim, working at the reception desk of the Daystar Hotel with not a notion of what she, Carrie, was going through here. That man had been not merely kissing her, but making love to her. Weakening her. She knew what the clamour in her body meant. If he came into the room at this minute, he could do what he liked with her and she wouldn't stop him. It had taken him only minutes to rouse her sexually to a degree she'd never experienced before. Paul had never done this to her, nor any other man. She'd been an innocent. She wasn't now.

With an effort she got up from the bed to change her clothes, tidy her hair—messed by his fingers. To make-up her face and hide that drowsy sexy look she knew intuitively was in her eyes. She pulled her shirt over her head, slipped out of the bra he'd unfastened and went to the wardrobe like someone in a daze. She'd wear her yellow cotton dress. It wasn't smart or elegant, but it would have to do.

She was reaching it down from its hanger when he opened the door and came into the room.

"What's taking you so long?"

She swung round, dropping the dress on the floor and crossing her arms to hide her half-naked body.

"Have you decided, like all women, that you haven't a thing to wear?" His eyes were mocking and he made no pretence that he wasn't looking at her nakedness. She stopped quickly, her face flaming, and picked up her dress to hold it in front of her shieldingly.

"I wish you'd leave me alone. I want to dress."

"Do you? Are you sure that's what you want, Carrie? Look at me." He said it so compellingly that she obeyed him, but she could stand his gaze for no more than a second or two. She knew too well that the heat of her desire was still smouldering in her eyes, and that a man of his experience wouldn't miss it.

"We'll make love some other time," he said mockingly as her eyes fell. "Put your dress on. Are you going to wear a bra?"

"Leave me alone," she said through her teeth. "I—I don't need your help and I don't want it."

"I believe you're modest," he commented dryly, and she felt tears come into her eyes.

"What if I am? Is there anything so wrong about that?"

"Not at all," he said. "I find it charming. I offered my help because you appear to be a little—distrait."

She bit her lip. "It's just that I'm relieved—about the cheque," she lied. "I've been worried sick. I'm all right now. If you'll go back to the sitting room, I shan't be ten minutes."

To her relief, he went.

Chapter Four

By the time she'd dressed and made up her face, she was feeling calmer, though scarcely less confused about her future. She told herself philosophically that she'd take it as it came, and went out to join him.

They lunched in the restaurant of one of the big waterside motels where there was a smorgasbord. Carrie was well aware today that people were looking at her, and she knew it was because of the company she was keeping. Feminine glances were inclined to slide over her disparagingly and then to move with more interest to Steve. He was obviously well known, but even those who didn't recognise him were aware of his charisma—and probably wondered why he was lunching with someone so unremarkable and ordinary. Possibly they saw her as a duty, or a poor relation, and though she was neither of these, she didn't feel in the least like his fiancée.

As they ate, he asked her casually, "Where would you like to be married, Carrie? Will Brisbane suit you? Or do you want a big do in Sydney?"

"Oh, no. I don't want a big wedding," she exclaimed. "But do we have to decide about it now? There's no great rush, is there?"

"No. But we're not putting it off indefinitely. As far as I'm concerned, the sooner the better, and you haven't given me any particular reason to believe you want to put it off too long, now the decision's been made." His eyes appraised her in an intimate sort of way, so that she knew he was thinking of her responses to him in Kim's flat, and she looked away from him embarrassed. "I mean," he went on dryly, "you don't have a job you must resign from—or parents who need to be convinced you know what you're doing in deciding to marry after so short an acquaintance."

Short? It was infinitesimal! She raised her eyes to his. "All the same, I would like to get to know you better before we marry," she said.

"Fair enough," he said, to her relief. "With exactly that in mind, I was going to suggest you should move into my apartment at the hotel some time tomorrow."

"Oh, no!" she exclaimed appalled. "I couldn't do that—not possibly."

"You could and you will," he said uncompromisingly. "And I'm not, contrary to what you may suspect, asking you to share my bed. I can control my passions, though yours appear inclined to get away from you. You'll have your own bedroom, your own bathroom, and if your aim is for us to get to know each other better, then it's an ideal solution."

"But Janelle Lane—and Miss Higgins—are there," she remarked futilely.

"So what? It's a large apartment."

"Have you told them about—us?" she asked after a moment.

"Not yet. I'll leave that until tomorrow, when you're there. . . . Have you finished with lunch? I'm taking you to Brisbane this afternoon. I want to buy you a ring, and I also want you to choose some new clothes for yourself."

"I don't need new clothes," she said quickly, unwilling to accept too many favours from him.

"Perhaps not, but I want you to have them." He got to his feet, and as she rose too, he told her, "If you won't choose what you want yourself, then I'll do it for you. So please yourself."

They left the restaurant followed by several pairs of curious eyes. If there'd been rumours along the Gold Coast that he was going to marry the beautiful Janelle Lane, then tongues would be wagging, and Carrie hoped there wouldn't be any gossip in the local papers.

As if he'd read her thoughts he told her, as he helped her into the car, "I'll put an announcement of our engagement in the newspapers in a day or two. Have you broken the news to your cousin?"

"In a—kind of a way," Carrie said awkwardly. They had started up the coast towards Southport.

"No doubt she was surprised. I hope she didn't warn you against me."

She gave him a quick look. "No. She thinks I should go ahead."

He smiled slightly. "Unlike you, your cousin

77

wouldn't need to have the advantages pointed out to her. From my knowledge of Kim, she wouldn't have turned down my proposal."

"You're flattering yourself," Carrie couldn't resist saying. "Kim has a boyfriend and she's perfectly satisfied with him."

"Even the most satisfactory of boyfriends don't always matter," he said cynically. "In my experience, the majority of women are out for what they can get. And I'm not flattering myself, it's not personal magnetism that attracts them in my case. It's money."

"Your money doesn't attract me in the least," Carrie exclaimed rashly, and he gave her a mocking smile.

"Then it must be my personality."

She blushed hotly. "Not that, either. You know why I've agreed to marry you, Mr. Revellion."

"Good heavens! How can you still call me that after practically begging me to seduce you this morning?"

Carrie thought she'd die of humiliation. "I did no such thing," she said, her voice scarcely audible.

"Then I must have misunderstood," he said blandly. "However, I'm pleased it's not my money that attracts you. I'd have thought it would be a real magnet to a big spender like you. So how is it you're so indifferent?"

Carrie leaned back and closed her eyes. It took an effort to remind herself she was supposed to be a big spender. She said tiredly, "I don't want to talk about it."

"I see. Well, you can spend all you want to this afternoon. And now what would you like to talk about?" She didn't answer and he asked, "Are you interested in live theatre? I've booked two seats for a show in Brisbane tonight."

She looked down at her yellow dress and grimaced. She loved the theatre, but this was hardly the dress to wear to it, besides he should have warned her. "I can't go," she said perversely. "Kim will be worried if I don't come home."

"Then for heavens sake—telephone her," he said sharply. "And if you're worrying about your clothes, I've told you we're going shopping."

He pulled up presently at a public phone box and Carrie rang Kim at the hotel. "I'm going to Brisbane with Steve and we'll be at a show tonight, so don't expect me to be in early."

"Great, I won't," Kim said. "Did you get it, Carrie? You know what I mean."

Oddly Carrie had forgotten all about the cheque. "Yes. I left it in the bedroom. It's in a plain envelope."

"Oh, thank heavens," Kim breathed. "You're marvellous, Carrie. I'll never stop being grateful to you. I'd have killed myself if you hadn't managed to get it, I really think I would. Have a great time tonight, won't you? You really deserve it. I'm so glad all this is happening for you—I'd have felt so mean and selfish otherwise. And thanks for ringing —I'd better go now."

Carrie hung up. Kim appeared to have conveniently forgotten that she was hardly delighted at what had happened—at the promise she'd had to make and was going to break. She went back to the car, and the handsome man who was waiting for her, and didn't care a thing about her personally.

He drove fast and expertly and they were in Brisbane in well under two hours. He took her first to a jeweller who was obviously expecting them, and introduced Carrie as "My fiancée, Miss Caroline Adams." In a private room, Carrie was shown a small selection of beautiful diamond rings, which the jeweller, Mr. Matheson, proceeded to slip onto her engagement finger in turn. Carrie had never owned a real diamond in her life, but for sure these were the genuine article and she felt bewildered as she examined their designs, trying to choose one. They all sparkled alluringly in the lights of the small room —both against the black velvet of the display case, and against the smooth, lightly tanned skin of her hands.

"Is there nothing there that really appeals to you, Carrie?" Steve asked at last. "Perhaps you'd prefer to have something specially made."

She hesitated. Perhaps it would delay things—but of course it would cost more. She didn't know what to do. She felt such a fraud. Finally, she asked him to choose for her.

He didn't argue and shortly after she left the shop with him, super-conscious of the beautiful ring that scintillated on her finger.

After that, they shopped, and Steve bought her more outfits than she'd ever had in her whole life. She had either to allow it or to create a scene in public, and that she was not prepared to do.

In the car again, he asked her, "Aren't you pleased about your new clothes? Most women would be—even fat and ugly women. You're one of the lucky ones who really can wear model clothes. It wouldn't take much to turn you into a beauty, in fact."

Carrie glanced at him suspiciously. That was nothing but flattery, she was certain—and yet flattery is pleasant. All the same, she couldn't bring herself to accept the compliment gracefully, or to do any more than thank him rather stiffly for his generosity. "I'm sorry, but I'm not used to having things bought for me," she added. "I don't really like it."

"Then you don't run true to form," he commented. "A girl who likes throwing her money around should take to this treatment like a duck to water."

He drove to one of the big hotels, where he'd reserved a small suite so that they could shower and change for dinner and the theatre. Carrie discovered that he'd actually arranged for a hairdresser to come and set her hair. The result, when she'd got into one of her new outfits, a very feminine dress of clinging black and white crepe de chine with a low cut back, was electrifying. But she was uneasy. She felt she was being drawn into a whirlpool from which there was no escape. And it was all so unreal, so much without heart. She was being groomed into a suitable partner for Steve Revellion. Love didn't come into it now and never would.

So he could hardly be surprised when she finally walked out on him, she told herself later on as she sat beside him in the theatre. He looked madly handsome in the dark suit and white shirt he'd brought with him in the car and changed into while she was showering. Glancing at him, she knew her feelings were very mixed—a hotchpotch of excitement and nervousness and guilt, impossible to deal with.

Though she'd suspected he might, he didn't suggest they should return to the hotel and spend the night there. After the theatre, they drove back down the coast. Carrie slept nearly all the way and woke

with a start when he pulled up outside Kim's flat.
Sleepily, she stumbled from the car with Steve's
hand under her arm. "I'll take your parcels to my
apartment," he told her. "You can move in any time
you like tomorrow—I'll probably call you around
noon, you should be fully conscious by then." He
lowered his head and kissed her lips briefly. "Good
night. I hope you've had a happy day."

It hadn't been too bad, and she mumbled her
thanks. Feeling dead tired she dragged herself up the
stairs and unlocked the front door of Kim's flat. She
was sound asleep before Kim came in late from her
date with Gene.

She woke next morning in time to breakfast with
her cousin who definitely wasn't one of those girls
who are satisfied with fruit juice and toast and a cup
of coffee. Kim had fresh papaw followed by bacon
and eggs and two slices of toast and marmalade.

"I could never eat all that," Carrie exclaimed,
joining her in the kitchen.

"Well, I've got my appetite back now, and I can't
work on an empty stomach," Kim said cheerfully.
"And please don't tell me it will make me fat. It suits
me to be a little bit plump—healthwise *and* where
looks are concerned. I look frightful with hollow
cheeks. But you have whatever you like, Carrie."

Carrie settled for papaw and toast and coffee, and
sat down at the small folding table opposite her.

Kim eyed her curiously. "Did you have a good
time last night?" she asked. Suddenly she noticed
the ring Carrie was wearing and seized her hand to
examine it. "Oh, Carrie—it's fabulous! It must have
cost the earth! Aren't you lucky!"

"You're forgetting I'll be giving it back," Carrie
said dryly, though she'd coloured.

"Must you? If I were you I'd go ahead and marry him."

"Kim, I hardly know him," Carrie said impatiently. "Would *you* rush off and marry someone you hardly knew?"

Kim grinned. "If he were as rich as Steve Revellion, I guess I would. As rich and as good looking *and* still only in his thirties—"

"*And* as hard as nails," Carrie added. "He's not even in love with me. He just wants a wife."

"Don't belittle yourself. He could have anyone. You're really pretty, Carrie—I like your new hairstyle by the way—and you have brains, too. He must be in love with you." She finished her second piece of toast and asked thoughtfully, "Is he passionate—even though he's hard as nails? I'll bet he is—"

Carrie coloured. "How on earth should I know?" she asked annoyed, though she knew very well that he was passionate, and in her opinion he was capable of turning it on for any girl if he chose to do so. "I do know that he likes his own way and that he's quite heartless, so don't talk to me about his being in love with me. He isn't."

Kim looked as if she knew better.

"Just don't be in a hurry to give that ring back," she advised. "And, speaking of hurrying—I'd better get moving. If I don't present myself at work on the dot, I'm likely to get the boot—even if I am your cousin! I picked up that cheque, by the way. It'll be in the post today. Am I relieved! It's like having a new lease on life—thanks to you. Will you be seeing Steve tonight?"

"Oh, I forgot to tell you," Carrie exclaimed. "He wants me to move into his apartment today—so we can get to know each other better. I'm sorry, Kim.

I'd much sooner stay here, but I don't see how I can get out of it."

"Don't worry about it!" Kim didn't look the least bit upset. "It's lovely having you here, of course, but—it could be a bit awkward. . . . Especially now when I want to make really sure of Gene. . . . So you won't be in to dinner?"

"No. I'm not looking forward to the move. Janelle Lane and her aunt are staying there, too, you know."

A little smile appeared on Kim's lips. "Why worry about that? To tell the truth, I could never stand Janelle Lane. She's always turning up at the Daystar —she used to come when old Mr. Revellion was still alive. She acts so important—you'd think she owned the place. I'd really like to see her face when she hears you're going to marry Steve Revellion."

Carrie didn't share her enthusiasm. In fact, she dreaded being presented to Janelle and her aunt as his fiancée. She wished futilely that they would leave the Gold Coast today and go back to Quaama Springs, or anywhere, so she wouldn't have to face them.

Carrie moved into Steve's apartment that afternoon. He sent a car to collect her and there was nothing she could do about it. She began to think she'd sold her soul, and to believe that Steve Revellion thought so too. The apartment was empty when she arrived, to her relief, but within minutes one of the housemaids came to see if she wanted her unpacking done, and to tell her that her new clothes had already been put away in the bedroom she was to use. Carrie was fully aware of the girl's envious and admiring glance at the ring she wore on her left hand, as she smiled at her and told her she could manage without any help.

Her bedroom was large and opulent, the carpet thick and soft, the furniture of a beautiful modern design. The adjoining bathroom was equipped with everything a woman could want, including bath salts, body cologne, exotic talcum powder and even a variety of cosmetics. Carrie had the feeling everything had been bought especially for her at Steve's instigation, and she didn't know how to take it. She felt curiously and ridiculously like a kept woman.

When the housemaid had gone she made a quick inspection of the apartment and found there were no less than five bedrooms, each, presumably, with its own bathroom. Besides the big room where he had interviewed her, there was a small intimate sitting room, and a separate dining room, also quite small. The kitchen was ultra modern and equipped with a large freezer as well as a refrigerator. From several of the windows, including her own, the view was spectacular. They looked out over the curling surf and the blue ocean to the limitless horizon, hazy with heat, and north and south along miles of sparkling white beach. Carrie went onto the balcony and found she was looking down into the hotel court, and the swimming pool there. Stretched out on one of the long padded loungers was Janelle Lane, flat on her back, tanning. Blissfully unaware of the news Steve would shortly be breaking to her.

She turned back and went inside feeling somehow guilty. But there was no quick way of extricating herself from the situation she was in. She'd simply have to wait till she turned twenty one and could pay off her—or Kim's—debts honourably.

In the course of unpacking her clothes, she discovered that the drawers of the chest were already stocked with beautiful brand new underthings, in her size, obviously ordered by Steve and rushed here ready for her coming, slips, panties, bras, in lilac, black and flesh. She heard her own helpless laugh. She didn't know whether she felt pampered or like a courtesan. *But after all,* she reasoned, *he does expect to marry me.*

Her belongings disposed of, she decided to go down to the beach. She certainly wasn't going to sit around here doing nothing and waiting for someone to turn up—particularly when the someone was as likely to be Janelle Lane as Steve. Spurning the two bikinis and the maillot with its plunging neckline and cut away sides that Steve had bought for her, she put on her yellow swimsuit that was two summers old and beginning to fade. She covered it with a velvety white towelling robe from the wardrobe, slipped her feet into thongs and went downstairs in the lift. Kim wasn't at the reception desk to her disappointment, so she went straight out to the beach where she spent the rest of the afternoon surfing and sunbaking. She could have been picked up at least three times, had she been interested, but she was in enough trouble already.

The apartment was no longer empty when she went back. As she let herself in she heard Janelle's voice, Steve's and Miss Higgins. All three of them were in the little sitting room having a pre-dinner drink.

"Is that you Carrie?" Steve called as she attempted to sneak past the door. "Come along in. I've been waiting for you."

Reluctantly, her heart thudding, she went into the

room. She was all too aware of her tumbled hair and the flush on her cheeks from her hours on the beach. There was salt on her lips and her lashes stuck together in salty points. Most of all, she wanted a shower.

Miss Higgins screwed up her round blue eyes and smiled at her in a puzzled way, and Janelle, a frosty glass in her hand, leaned back in her chair, merely turning her head to send Carrie a cold, unfriendly look. Steve rose to come across the room to put his arm around her and draw her over to the others.

It was sundown, and the eastern sky was flooded with red and gold clouds streaming across it. A warm, dramatically coloured light fell across the balcony and into the room so that both Carrie and Steve, as they moved forward, stepped into it. Carrie's white robe changed to flame. Glancing up at the man beside her she was startled at the effect the light had on his face, turning its tan into gilded bronze, firing his blue eyes with a red light, scintillating in his hair. He wore a cream shirt with the sleeves rolled up and well-fitting light beige pants that seemed moulded to his narrow hips.

He drew Carrie against him and said almost abruptly, "Nella, Janelle, I want you to be the first to know that Carrie's promised to marry me."

Carrie felt shock rock along her nerves and the blood come to her face. Janelle's pale blue eyes had widened with hostility and disbelief, and Miss Higgins looked so comically and exaggeratedly astounded, Carrie almost laughed. Her eyes were stretched wide, round in her round face, and her small mouth had fallen open on a gasp of surprise.

There was a ghastly moment of silence, and then

Miss Higgins exclaimed in a high-pitched voice, "Steve, you're playing a joke on us!"

"Indeed I'm not, Nella," Steve said pleasantly. "You should know me better than to believe I'd play that kind of a joke."

Janelle was staring and biting savagely at her lower lip. *She'd like to tear me to pieces,* Carrie thought, wishing she could sink through the floor. She was furious with Steve for his brutally blunt statement that plainly left Janelle speechless with shock, and she couldn't help feeling a certain sympathy for the other girl. Suppose Paul had chosen this way to tell her that it was the end of everything between them—with Josie Tanner actually there, in his arms and listening? She'd have died! It was cruel and utterly heartless. Didn't he care who he hurt— or how much he hurt them? She wished wildly that she could contradict his statement, tell Miss Higgins that she was quite right, it was all a joke.

Meanwhile Nella Higgins was saying, her voice shriller than ever, "I—I just can't believe it! Why, we've only met this girl once—and the next thing you're telling us she's going to marry you. Why, I thought you and Janelle . . ."

"Be quiet, Nella, for goodness sake," Janelle broke in. Her pale blue eyes went to Carrie, snaking over her rapidly from head to toe in a venomous way. "Congratulations, Carrie. When's the wedding to be?"

Carrie turned to Steve, incapable of answering that question, and he said, "We'll let you know, Janelle, never fear." Then to Carrie's embarrassment, he touched his lips to her brow, murmuring, "Won't we, darling?"

She stood as if she were turned to stone, rigid and unresponsive. He pushed the hair back from her forehead. "You taste of salt, dearest. Did you enjoy your swim?"

"Yes, thank you," she said stiltedly. She felt like a member of the audience dragged onto the stage and ordered to play a part. She didn't even know her lines, and what was more, the audience was decidedly hostile. Her gaze had settled on Steve's mouth, she couldn't make herself look at those mercilessly searching eyes of his, and she could see the cynical, almost cruel tilt of its line. The pressure of his fingers on her shoulder seemed to be warning her, "Play up! I'm paying you six thousand dollars for this." Well, she couldn't play up and she couldn't even smile.

With an effort she pulled away from him. "I'd better go and take a shower and dress."

"I guess you had," he drawled, his eyes lingering on her. "Put on that violet silk affair. We're not going out tonight."

Carrie cast one quick look at the other two women and somehow managed to get herself through the door and into her own room. She closed the door and leaned against the wall. She felt absolutely terrible. How on earth had she imagined she was going to act as if she were his fiancée? What was worse, how was she going to last out for over a month? Heaven knew when Janelle Lane would leave here, but she had a nasty feeling it wouldn't be soon. It wouldn't worry Steve—he didn't care a fig for anyone's feelings. But it was going to worry her. She put her hands to her face and wished futilely she'd never got herself into this situation—but what other way had there been to help Kim?

The door opened and closed, and she heard Steve's voice ask harshly, "Well, what's bothering you now?"

"What do you think?" She took her hands from her face and glared at him. Behind him, the red sunset light flooded across the pale walls, the pale carpet, and painted the big bed crimson. She looked away from it quickly. "Did you expect me to enjoy that little scene? When there've been all those rumours about you and Janelle."

His lips curled. "Most women I know would have wallowed in it. There's nothing a woman likes more than to triumph over some other female."

"Oh, you think you know so much about women, don't you?" she snapped. "Personally, I think you have a warped mind. I didn't wallow in it—I *loathed* it. I hate that kind of shock treatment. Don't you have any sensitivity? Did you have to say I was going to marry you?"

"For Pete's sake—why not?" he said angrily. "What did you want me to say?"

"You could have told them I'd come to stay for awhile, let Janelle get used to—seeing me around." She looked at him aggressively and he looked back at her, his level blue gaze aiming right at the centre of her being. Or that was how it felt, and she lowered her lashes quickly as if to hide from him.

"Special treatment for Janelle," he said. "You think it's a good idea to let a shark get used to the fact there's a nice little fish swimming around, do you?"

"How can *you* talk about sharks?" she flashed, and glancing up saw his nostrils whiten.

"We made a bargain," he said coldly.

"*You* dictated the no-alternative terms," she retorted.

"You didn't have to accept them," he reminded her. "That was your choice entirely."

"You know that's not true," she said passionately. "You know I had to accept."

"Don't try to tear at my heartstrings," he said cynically. "Why not give in and admit you're onto a good thing? As I said before, you've won the jackpot. I don't imagine for a moment that Kim thinks its tough on you. Wouldn't she change places with you if she had the chance?"

"Oh, you and your opinion of women! You think we're all so mercenary," Carrie said angrily.

"That's right, I do. . . . However, one thing's for sure, you're in this now right up to your neck, so make up your mind to learn to live with it. You may find in time you even like it."

"I doubt it," Carrie said.

They stared at each other. The room was rapidly growing dark, all the rich red colour had faded. Along the coast, lights were beginning to gleam yellow-white against the darkening sea. Carrie moved nervously across to the windows to stare out and to wish she were back in her own tiny flat in Sydney. Now she knew how it felt to be a rabbit caught in a trap—but she was going to escape. She knew it wouldn't be easy, but she'd simply have to be ruthless and play dirty. He trampled on other people's feelings, she reminded herself. He didn't deserve any consideration.

She heard him move, and was aware of the warmth of his body even before he put his arms around her, crossing them over her breasts and pulling her back against him. She felt the swift beat of her own heart as she forced herself not to struggle, but could barely refrain from remarking bitterly, "This is part of the agreement, I suppose."

"*Everything*'s in the contract," he reminded her.

For a moment she wondered just how far he'd be prepared to go, and what her chances were of keeping their physical relationship within decent limits during the next few weeks. It had seemed possible enough when Kim had suggested she should play along with him, but now she knew it was going to be a battle, and her heart thudded at the thought.

He was still holding her against him, and now, feeling the quickening of her heartbeats, he pushed aside her robe and slipped his hands inside the top of her swimsuit to stroke her breasts. "You should be wearing one of those little bikinis we bought in Brisbane," he said softly against her ear. "I like the feel of your skin under my hands and this thing's restrictive."

Carrie pulled away from his sharply. "Leave me alone! I'm not married to you yet."

"Now exactly what's that supposed to mean?" His arm reached out to catch at her robe and pull it half off her as she tried to slither away. She stood breathing quickly, half frightened by the anger that blazed from his eyes and the ugly expression on his sensual mouth.

"It means just what it says," she said, swallowing nervously.

"You think I shouldn't touch you till we're married, is that it? Well you've given me your promise and as far as I'm concerned that's unalterable. No harm would be done if I threw you on that bed and made love to you now. A few days, a few weeks, I don't see that it makes any difference."

"Well, *I* do," she quavered.

His eyes mocked her. "I can't believe you're as old-fashioned as that, Carrie."

She bit her lip. "But I am."

He ignored that and with narrowed eyes, he reached out to switch on a wall lamp so he could search her face. She tried to pull the robe back onto her shoulders but with a swift movement he dragged it down over her arms and tossed it to the floor. She stood before him in her faded yellow swimsuit. She felt naked as his eyes raked over her, lingering on every detail of her figure. She had no idea what to expect, and uttered a faint gasp of relief when he told her, "Get ready for your shower." He strode across the room to flick on another light, then took the long violet gown from the wardrobe and flung it on the bed. "You'll wear this. From now on, you can forget your old clothes and start looking as if you were about to marry me—and acting that way, too. So see you put on a good performance at dinner. No standing on the sidelines while I play your part for you. I want six thousand dollars worth of value from you, Carrie, starting right now."

"And you talk about women being mercenary!" she breathed. "You haven't bought me, you know, Mr. Revellion."

"Don't call me that again," he said threateningly. "As for buying you—I think I have. When I say jump, you're to jump."

"How high?" she asked angrily, her dark eyes smouldering.

"Over the moon, if I say so. You're up to your eyes in debt to me, and don't you forget it."

"I'm not likely to, with you cracking the whip around my ears all the time," she flung back, suddenly close to tears. "You didn't tell me it was part of the bargain to have you treat me as if—as if I were a circus animal. I'm beginning to hate you."

The fire went out of his eyes and he looked utterly weary.

"I apologise. But I don't like being cheated. Remember that." He turned on his heel and left the room, closing the door behind him.

Carrie's shoulders drooped. Across the room she caught sight of her reflection in the big wall mirror, forlorn and yet a little wanton in her old swimsuit, her hair tumbled, her cheeks hectic, her dark eyes shining. From what she knew of Steve Revellion, she concluded that his dislike of being cheated had something, probably a great deal, to do with the girl who had jilted him. Practically at the altar, Kim had said. That was why he was so hard and unfeeling now. It was difficult to believe that a man with so much personal charisma, so much arrogance and self-confidence, had actually been *jilted*. Yet it was going to happen again, when she walked out on him. The thought troubled her. Somewhere at the back of her mind was the suspicion that if he had chosen to woo her, to be persuasive and charming, as he was very occasionally, she might have really liked him, liked him in fact, very much . . . As it was, she'd really meant it when she'd said she was beginning to hate him. Or did she? It was all very confusing.

She turned away from her reflection and stepped out of her suit. She'd take a long relaxing shower and she wouldn't think about him any more. It was too exhausting.

Chapter Five

Carrie tried to behave in the way that was expected of her at dinner that night, though it was undeniably a strain in the company of Janelle and her aunt. Janelle wore an elegant black gown that contrasted with her blonde hair, and Nella Higgins's dumpy little figure was draped in milk coffee georgette. Carrie, aware she had surprised them with her sophisticated violet hostess gown, tried to disregard the awkwardness of the situation and simply enjoy the dinner that was served from the hotel kitchen. Food, after all, was her field, and her specialised training at the Catering College enabled her to assess and to appreciate both the dishes and the presentation. When she voiced her approval of the sauce that accompanied the chicken they were eating, however, Janelle practically jumped on her.

"Really, Carrie, we all know the food's good here. Do we have to talk about it?"

Carrie flushed, but Steve came to her rescue with a drawled out, "Personally, Jan, I find talking about it is half the pleasure."

Chagrined, Janelle bit her lip, then rallied quickly. "Well, that's if you know something about it. Now I do. In fact, Max used to say that I was something of a gourmet. Do you remember that, Steve? You must have heard him. Whenever we went to Brisbane or Sydney—and especially in Singapore or Hong Kong—I always used to insist on trying dishes I hadn't tasted before." She looked at Carrie in a supercilious way across the table. "I should imagine you're too young and inexperienced to know much about fine food or good wines. You have a lot to learn. What are you? Eighteen?"

"I'm a little older than that," Carrie said as pleasantly as she could manage. "And food and drink are not mysteries to me."

"My little fiancée, in fact, is very well clued up when it comes to such things," Steve cut in before she could say anything further. "It's possible she knows more about cuisine than any of us, so I'd advise you to be careful what you say, Jan."

Janelle looked furious. "I wasn't going to say a thing, Steve. Your chef has always been irreproachable." Immediately after that, she introduced a topic of which she knew Carrie was ignorant—Steve's cattle holding on the Darling Downs, talking about the aftermath of the drought, the problems of soil erosion and water run off.

"That nice young man from the C.S.I.R.O. came to see us a few weeks ago," she told Steve. "He was really fascinated to see how well we're recovering from those tremendous storms we had last summer. Lots of our neighbors have had their paddocks washed away, but, as you well know, Max was always supersensitively aware of the dangers of soil erosion—'' Jan paused briefly to shoot Carrie a quick and maliciously triumphant glance. It said plainly to the recipient that she could hardly hope to compete in the conversation.

Janelle is talking as though she owned the property, Carrie thought, *yet she is only the widow of the former manager and is only allowed to remain there because of Steve's father, and now Steve's generosity.*

"I think you should take some of the credit for our good fortune, too," Janelle continued, throwing Steve an arch glance. "I remember Max saying that when you worked with him at Quaama Springs you insisted on putting into practice all sorts of revolutionary ideas you'd learned at agricultural college.

"I'd hardly call them revolutionary," Steve said with a pleasant smile. "But I've always been interested in land uses and conservation. Max and I worked as a team—he had practical experience, I had a few new ideas, and we got on very well together the five years I was there. I sometimes think I'd have been there still if my father hadn't been warned to take things more easily, and I hadn't had to more or less take over and apply myself to hotels and land development."

"And to make a fortune," Nella simpered.

"You were wasted in the bush, Steve," Janelle said, then asked Carrie abruptly, "Where are you from, Carrie?"

"From Sydney," Carrie said. She'd been reflecting that she was learning one or two things about her fiancé tonight. She hadn't know that he'd been to agricultural college and worked at Quaama Springs, but now, on consideration, she could see him quite easily in the role of cattleman, riding a horse in the blazing sunlight, branding, mustering, sleeping under the stars. Rough and tough. Oddly, it made him much more of a real person to her.

After dinner, Nella turned on the television set and settled herself in an armchair to watch the programme she'd selected. Steve took Carrie's arm. "You haven't seen my swimming pool up on the roof, yet, Carrie. Come and I'll show it to you."

"But Steve!" Nella exclaimed. "Can't that wait? I mean—this Spanish drama on Channel O should be well worth watching."

"Then you and Janelle must go ahead and watch it, my dear Nella," Steve said. "Don't let what Carrie and I are doing interfere with your plans." He urged Carrie toward the door. Janelle shot her a venomous glance.

Certainly it was beautifully peaceful up on the roof of the hotel at night. This apparently was Steve's private swimming pool and Carrie wondered why Janelle hadn't been sunbathing up here today, instead of down on the hotel terrace. Perhaps she didn't have access to the pool, though it was more likely she preferred to be seen and admired instead of hiding herself away up here. It would be different if Steve were around.

"You can bathe in the nude here, if you wish," Steve said.

His arms was about her and she tensed and said quickly, "I don't care to bathe in the nude, thank you."

"I didn't mean now," he said sardonically. "During the day, when I'm attending to my business affairs. You're going to have plenty of time for it in the next few days, I'm afraid. Things didn't go as well as I'd hoped today."

Great, Carrie thought unsympathetically. *She didn't want to have to spend any more time with him than she had to.* She moved away from him to look out over the mysterious dark ocean, glinting in the starlight, and up at the vast sky and the bright stars that seemed so close and yet were millions of miles away. She'd heard it said that in the outback the stars seemed to come right down to meet you, and though the Darling Downs were scarcely in the outback, the thought made her ask him, "Did you really like working on your cattle station, Steve?"

"Sure I liked it. But with my father's health the way it was, I couldn't stay there. I didn't want him to drop dead because of my self indulgence." He had come to join her, to lean on the ledge and look with her along the beach, where the white foam made endless scatterings of lace as the sea came surging in. "I gather you're a city girl."

"Yes," she said, and hesitated. "I think I'd like to live in the country though. It's funny, but Janelle doesn't seem like a country woman."

"She's not," he said. "She's a Brisbane lady. She was transplanted when she married Max Lane."

"Oh. She's very keen on Quaama Springs, isn't she? She—she knows all about it."

He moved abruptly and pulled her into his arms. "What does all that matter? I didn't bring you up here to talk about Janelle."

"Then what did you bring me here for?" she breathed, stirred in spite of herself by his nearness.

"This," he said. His mouth touched hers, gently at first, and then he was kissing her roughly, passionately. She was weak and breathless when he let her go, and she discovered with a shock that Janelle had come to join them on the roof.

As Steve had warned her, he was fully occupied during the next few days. Certainly he was there for dinner, but he was remote and abstracted, and Carrie felt, not without a certain sense of relief, that their relationship was at a standstill. She kept out of Janelle's way as much as she could, and when she wasn't on the beach, she went to Kim's flat where she read or lazed or listened to music—and marked off the days to her twenty-first birthday on the calendar that hung on the kitchen wall. Janelle nevertheless managed to lead her to understand that she was in Steve's confidence, and that she knew all about the problem that was absorbing his time and energy.

"Steve's having a fight with the company about the last parcel of land they've acquired, and what restrictions there are going to be on its use," she said offhandedly at breakfast one day when Steve had gone early, before anyone was up. She looked at Carrie in a sneering way. "I suppose you're feeling neglected. You wouldn't understand his dedication to his work."

Carrie didn't answer. As a matter of fact, Steve had left a note on the dressing table—he must have put it there while she was asleep—telling her he was going to Brisbane and wouldn't be in till after dinner that night. For once, Carrie felt rebellious, though she was not quite sure why. It wasn't as if she wanted to go to Brisbane with him, she certainly didn't—or so she told herself. But to have Janelle lording it over her at the breakfast table, pointing up how much she knew about Steve and his affairs and how little Carrie knew, was just too much. Carrie felt she couldn't get away from her fast enough, and as soon as she could she went downstairs to reception to see if Kim was about. She was there at the desk alone, looking quite cheerful, though dark shadows under her eyes suggested she'd been having late nights.

"Hi, Carrie," she greeted her cousin cheerfully. "How's it going? How are you getting on with the snakey Mrs. Lane?"

Carrie grimaced. "Not terribly well. I'm just about coping."

"And what about Steve Revellion? Have you changed your mind about not going through with it? Oh, I have a letter for you." She reached under the desk and produced it. "It's from Paul Stanhope, he's put his name on the back. Didn't you say you and he were through?"

Carrie nodded. She had given very little thought to Paul the last few days. She'd had other things on her mind. As she took the letter from Kim she said vaguely, "I suppose he wants to tell me the latest news—about a job he hoped to get, that's all."

"Not as interesting as your news," Kim said brightly. "Look, I'm off this afternoon. If you have nothing else to do, why don't we go down to the beach?"

"Great," Carrie agreed, and as a small group of people drifted toward the reception desk, she left Kim to deal with them. Crossing the lobby, she went through to the terrace that surrounded the swimming pool. She sat down at one of the tables in the shade of a big beach umbrella and opened Paul's letter. For some strange reason she found she didn't really want to hear from Paul.

Carrie Darling,

I rang you the other day as I promised I would, and when you didn't answer I dropped by, only to be told by the people downstairs that you'd flown off to the Gold Coast. You certainly didn't lose much time going after that millionaire, did you? Maybe you've had better luck than I have. Mine has run right out. My talk with Frank Tanner was a complete fizz. He's nothing more than a hard-headed business man and he wanted all kinds of guarantees that I couldn't give, so after about an hour, he said a polite goodbye and showed me to the door and that was that. Well, I had to give it a fly, but now it's back to square one. I'm planning on coming up to Surfers in a week or so and I hope you and I will be able to work out something exciting together. I was crazy saying what I did the other night.

Ever yours, Paul

P.S. Hang on to that legacy—we're going to need it!

Carrie raised her head and stared at the blue waters of the pool. She was finding it difficult to take in what Paul's letter said—or implied. He was coming up here to join her in about a week! She couldn't believe it and—she didn't want to. How different it would have been if Kim hadn't rung her that night, and she hadn't rushed off to Surfers Paradise the next morning! She'd have been home when he rang then, and by now—would she have found it easy to forgive him?

She read the letter through again and though she knew she should be thrilled, she wasn't. It was largely because the thought of having him come here was so disturbing. It would create an absolutely impossible situation while she was so involved with Steve Revellion. But as well as that, she was too conscious of the things his letter hadn't said. Not a word of apology for how he had hurt her, nothing to say that he had ever loved her. Not a word either about Josie Tanner, the elegant blue-eyed blonde. Had he finished with her? Had her attraction stemmed mainly from the fact her father could offer him a big career opportunity? That hadn't come off obviously because Frank Tanner had discovered Paul's own lack of finance. So was her own attraction no deeper than the legacy she had coming up? And if something better turned up?

Now she was being really cynical. She'd never have dreamed of thinking that way about Paul once.

Frowning, she looked up into the face of another elegant blonde, whose light blue eyes were concealed behind huge sunglasses. Janelle Lane. How long had she been standing there?

She dropped down into a chair near Carrie's.

"I didn't know the mail had come. Or is that an old love letter you're reading?"

Carrie blushed hotly. "What makes you think it's a love letter?"

"Masculine writing, my dear—plus that look on your face," Janelle said. "Who is he?" She lit a cigarette and tossed back her head as she drew on it. She was wearing a revealing black maillot and she looked fetching enough to draw the attention of several males. Carrie, neat in white jeans and sea-blue shirt, felt comparatively invisible.

"Well?" Janelle said.

"Do you usually ask people you scarcely know questions about their private correspondence?" Carrie heard herself ask.

Janelle laughed throatily. "No, I don't, darling. But though I scarcely know you, I do know the man you've managed to get yourself engaged to. I know him *very well*. But I don't expect you to answer my question—not truthfully, anyway. You look green enough, but I suspect that under that little girl exterior there's a clever scheming woman. . . . However, if you only knew—you're not nearly as shrewd or clever as you imagine you are."

Carrie stared at her, repelled and fascinated. She'd never had to deal with anyone like this before. Janelle's eyes were still hidden behind the sunglasses, but her painted mouth smiled and smiled. There was no denying her beauty, though in the bright light of the sunshine, there were little lines, little signs of coarseness, in her face that were imperceptible indoors. She was over thirty, Carrie decided—quite a few years over. And hence, a whole lot more experienced than she was. Not that that would be hard. Carrie didn't pretend she'd been around much, and as for imagining herself shrewd or clever, Paul's treatment of her had proved she was scarcely that. As she stared at Janelle her hands were busy folding Paul's letter—putting it out of sight in its envelope, though with her mind she was scarely aware of it.

"Don't you want to know why I say you're not as clever as you think?" Janelle asked, still smiling.

"Not particularly," Carrie said, wishing she could get up and walk away. "Because actually I don't think I'm clever."

Janelle laughed. "What? You've managed to get yourself engaged to Steve Revellion and you don't think you're clever? I don't suppose you'll tell me how you did it."

"No," Carrie agreed coolly though inwardly she was shaking. "I won't tell you."

"Then I'll guess. You told him you were pregnant."

Carrie thought she was going to be sick. "I haven't—" She stopped abruptly. She wasn't going to make explanations or discuss it in any way.

"You haven't known him that long," Janelle mocked. "Well, I'd guessed that. How long have you known him?"

Carrie didn't answer. She had no idea what Steve had told Janelle—if anything—about their acquaintance. For the first time, she was really conscious of her youth, her innocence, and she felt herself curiously at the mercy of the older woman.

"I have the feeling you're almost brand new around here," Janelle said. She tapped ash from her cigarette and smiled at a man who was staring at her. "How much has Steve told you about me?"

"What do you mean?" Carrie's dark eyes were wary. Steve had been guarded. He'd said he'd thought about marrying Janelle, and he'd said he wasn't going to do so, and that was about all.

"I mean, did he tell you we'd been lovers for quite some time? And he wants me to marry him."

Carrie bit her lip, aware of shock. He'd told her

nothing of having been Janelle's lover. But then she could hardly have expected that he would. With a feeling of distaste, she said calmly, "That doesn't make sense. If he wants to marry you, he'd hardly have asked me, would he?" She was unconsciously twisting the diamond ring around on her finger, and Janelle laughed huskily.

"It's a little more complicated than that. I know he asked you and obviously you jumped at it. But that gorgeous ring doesn't mean a thing, Carrie. Engaged isn't married, and the only reason you're engaged to Steve, my dear, is because I refused him. In fact, it's all a bit of bluff for my benefit. Don't think you're anything special—Steve could have chosen anyone, so long as they were handy and willing." She drew slowly on her cigarette, blew smoke, and then asked lazily, "Do you want to hear about it? Or do you prefer to remain in blissful ignorance?"

Carrie's heart was beating uncomfortably fast. She was already aware that Steve thought one woman would do as well as another, but if Janelle only knew, Carrie hadn't exactly jumped at the chance of becoming engaged to him, and what was more, she had no intention of marrying him. She still had no idea what Janelle was talking about, and of course she was curious—anyone would have been—but she was determined not to show it. She disliked Janelle intensely and she wished she'd never met her.

The sun had climbed higher up in the sky and the shade had shifted, and Carrie, who didn't want blisters on her nose, moved her chair a little before she said off-handedly, "No, I don't want to hear about it, Janelle. I can get along quite well being blissfully ignorant."

The other girl's mouth tightened with anger. "Then I should leave you to wallow in it, if that's what you think. But believe me, it would be unkind. Steve doesn't care how much you get hurt. He's notoriously callous where most women are concerned, in case you hadn't noticed it. But I'm going to be generous and warn you."

"Warn me of what?" Carrie asked it without meaning to, and squirmed at the look of triumph on Janelle's face.

"That one day, right out of the blue, he'll tell you to pack your things and vamoose."

Carrie almost asked why, but just managed to stop herself in time. She didn't know what Janelle was talking about, but suppose Steve did tell her that—it would suit her quite well, though she wouldn't tell Janelle so. And it would be fair enough, if it was what he wanted to do. Heaven knew, he was paying her enough; he could surely please himself.

"I'll tell you why," Janelle said, though Carrie hadn't asked her. "It's because, eventually, he's going to marry me. There's nothing surer. I refused him once, but he'll be back. For once in his life, he's going to have to give in to a woman."

Carrie listened, skeptically. As far as she was concerned, Janelle was still talking in riddles, but when it came to Steve's giving in to a woman, she simply didn't believe it. Nor did she think he was sufficiently in love with Janelle to give in to her over anything. One woman was as good as another. That was his motto.

"You don't believe me, do you?" Janelle was

saying. "But you will in a moment. You see, if he doesn't marry me within the next five months, he'll lose Quaama Springs. It will be mine. It's all set out in his father's will. Steve's steered clear of matrimony ever since he had an affair that went sour on him, and of course Tony wanted him to marry and produce heirs." She paused to light another cigarette. "So, knowing how Steve loves Quaama Springs, Tony left it to him only on condition that he and I marry within twelve months of his death. If not—then it's mine."

"But why did you refuse him?" Carrie stammered out bewilderedly, trying to take it all in. The things she didn't know! Her ignorance—blissful or otherwise—of the man to whom she was ostensibly engaged seemed to be abysmal.

"For the simple reason that I don't want to spend the rest of my life in the bush," Janelle said. "Steve's big idea at the moment is to get out of Revellion-West and live at Quaama Springs, which to my mind would be madness. He'd be bored to extinction in a matter of weeks. I've told him this, but he hates to be told anything, especially by a woman." Janelle leaned back in the chair and smiled meditatively. "He imagines that by getting himself engaged to some girl—any girl—you, as it happens—he can frighten me into submission. But he can't." She dropped her hand to ash her cigarette on the ground. "He's the one who's going to have to give in this time, or he'll lose his precious cattle station altogether."

Carrie's attention was riveted on her. So this was what it was all about! It had seemed quite inexplicable that Steve had asked her to marry him just because he wanted a wife, but now she was beginning to understand what was behind it all. And while she couldn't have cared less that she would never be Steve's wife, she loathed having Janelle Lane tell her so in her triumphantly sneering way, and she loathed it even more when Janelle drawled out, "So do you see now why you can kiss your dreams of becoming Mrs. Steven Revellion a sweet good-bye, Carrie darling? My only advice to you is, if you haven't seduced him already, then don't. You'll only hurt yourself."

Carrie's cheeks flushed. Seduce him! She wouldn't know how to seduce a man if her life depended on it. And the way things were going, it was far more likely that he would seduce her. But perhaps this was just Janelle's unpleasant way of putting things. By this time, she'd heard all she wanted and more, but before she went she was going to say something to wipe that smug look off Janelle Lane's face. Quite frankly, she couldn't imagine Steve giving in to any woman for any reason, and while Janelle was obviously in a strong position, Carrie still thought Janelle would be the one who had to back down—if she really wanted him, and it seemed that she did. And that was why he went on about expecting Carrie to give a good performance. He was going to frighten Janelle into giving in.

Carrie got to her feet and said calmly, "Thank you for your advice, Janelle. I'm sure you mean well, but I have some to offer you too, if I may."

"Really?" Janelle surveyed her icily. "Well, I don't think it will be worth hearing, but let's have it."

"Just don't be too sure of yourself," Carrie said. "I really don't think you're going to find it all that easy to get the better of Steve. . . . And now if you'll excuse me, I must go. Has Miss Higgins gone out, or is she still in the apartment?"

"I haven't a clue," Janelle snapped. "If you're all that interested, you can find out for yourself." Then as Carrie turned away she said sneeringly, "I suppose you're silly enough to think he's as much in love with you as you obviously are with him."

Carrie kept walking, her blood pounding through her veins. She reached the cool shade of the hotel lobby and crossed to the lifts. That—that beastly female! But she wasn't going to make an exhibition of herself by saying she wasn't in love with him. Oh, it was funny really. He didn't mean to marry her at all, and she'd been feeling so guilty about playing dirty, when that was exactly what he was going to do. Though she—or Kim at least, would be six thousand dollars better off.

The lift came and she stepped into it, and pressed the button for the fourteenth floor. Unexpectedly, her knees had begun to tremble, and her mind was full of confusion. The thought of having to face Nella Higgins was suddenly intolerable. She had to do some thinking. Not only about what Janelle had told her, but about Paul too, especially now that everything had changed. She pressed the button for the first floor. There was a lounge there. Or would it be better to go to the beach? But if she did, she'd need her hat, her sunglasses and they were in the apartment. What a mess she was in! And all because she'd let Janelle get under her skin.

And because of hearing from Paul, she reminded herself.

It was at that point she discovered she didn't have his letter. It wasn't on the floor, so she must have dropped it in the lobby or out by the pool. Well, that settled the problem of which floor she wanted.

She didn't find the letter. It wasn't on the floor in the lobby and it wasn't out by the pool, and Janelle was no longer there. So either it had been tidied up by one of the staff or Janelle had rescued it. Carrie hoped it was the former.

Chapter Six

Sheltering under a big green umbrella she'd hired, Carrie spent the rest of the morning on the beach. Some of the time she thought about Steve Revellion and what Janelle had told her. Some of the time, lulled by the roar of the sea, the glitter of the sun on the water, she mindlessly watched the sunbakers, the surfers, the ball games, the lovemaking. And now and again she thought about Paul. She didn't know what she felt about Paul. But the fact that he might be here in a few days time was definitely disturbing. If he turned up now, she'd never be able to explain the mess she was in, it was far too complicated.

Exactly what had he said in his letter? It was infuriating that she'd lost it. But whatever she felt, whatever she wanted—and she was sure about neither—she'd have to write and tell him not to come. She couldn't possibly walk out on Steve yet. Her conscience wouldn't allow it. Or she thought it was her conscience. She was determined to pay him back the money she owed him first, though now it seemed possible he might get in ahead of her and tell her it was all over. She wondered why he hadn't told her at the beginning that it was all no more than a charade. Probably he thought she'd put on a better show if she really believed he was going to marry her. *Why me?* she wondered. And now she knew. He'd chosen Carrie Adams because she was so young and naïve and unsuspecting, and she wasn't emcumbered with parents who might make a fuss.

One thing was for sure, and that was, he didn't believe in half measures. Recalling her few sexual encounters with him, she admitted with a feeling of fear that he could quite easily seduce her, if he wanted to. He was a man of experience, and possibly cynical enough to take it that the loss of her virginity would be amply compensated for by the gain of a few thousand dollars—plus a diamond ring and a new wardrobe. It wasn't a happy thought, and lying face down in the sand, her cheek resting on her forearm, she admitted to herself that she'd lost faith in men since Paul had dropped her so callously. In a strange way, it seemed to her that she might as well marry the way she was marrying, for reasons completely unconnected with emotions, love and trust. There would have to be respect, of course, and a certain amount of cooperation and tolerance. And eventually, out of that, wasn't it possible that—

She sat up, blinking. She must be falling asleep. She wasn't going to marry Steve at all. He was going to marry Janelle.

Later she left the beach and wandered onto Cavill Avenue and across the plaza to MacDonalds where she had a large and succulent hamburger. Hardly the kind of lunch the future wife of Steve Revellion would be expected to eat, she reflected wryly, but then she wasn't the future wife of Steve Revellion, and anyhow, she only had a couple of dollars with her. It was a comfort to know that Kim was free that afternoon and she wouldn't have to go back to the hotel apartment till after dinner. The longer she could put off seeing Janelle again, the better she would be.

She and Kim spent the whole afternoon on the beach. Kim loaned Carrie a bikini she'd grown out of, as she put it euphemistically, and they had a lazy time, both of them sleeping a little in between swims.

"I suppose you'll have to shoot off back to the hotel soon and get dressed up to go to some fabulous restaurant for a fabulous meal," Kim remarked as they left the surf after a final swim. She seemed to have conveniently forgotten that Carrie was far from enthusiastic about her relationship with Steve Revellion, and could see him only as an enviable catch.

"Actually, no," Carrie said. "He—Steve won't be in till after dinner tonight. Do you have a date with Gene?"

"Not tonight."

They'd reached the place where they'd left their surf towels and nearby two young men were eyeing them. Carrie rather quickly enveloped herself in her towel, but Kim was not so modest, and concentrated on tossing her wet hair back from her face, and obviously enjoyed the interested glances of the males. Then she turned her back on the two suntanned men and mouthed, "They want to pick us up. Shall we let them?"

Carrie shook her head. She didn't want to be

picked up. She wasn't wearing her diamond ring. She'd left it tucked away at the back of a drawer in Kim's bedroom. It was far too valuable to wear into the surf. "I was going to ask if I could have dinner at your place, but of course if you'd rather—" She rolled her eyes and gestured with her head.

"We could ask them along, too," Kim said in an undertone.

Carrie shook her head again, feeling disappointed. "Not for me. But you go ahead. I'll eat in a café somewhere, I don't want to go back to the hotel for a while yet."

Kim made a comical face. "I can't handle two on my own. Okay, we'll go back to the flat. I just hope I'm not unknowingly passing up a chance to meet up with a millionaire who'd fall in love with me on sight. But I guess it doesn't happen twice in the same family—like lightning and all that. . . . Tell me what the letter from your ex-boyfriend was about, by the way," she went on as they walked across the sand to one of the narrow paths through the dunes.

"He's talking of coming up here," Carrie said uneasily. "I think he wants me back."

"As if you'd go back to him now!" Kim scoffed. "Oh, I know you carried on when you first got engaged, but I know you've been having second thoughts about it, haven't you?"

"Definitely not," Carrie said emphatically, as they made their way along the Esplanade. "But all the same, I can't just disappear with Paul when I owe Steve all that money—even if I wanted to."

"And you don't want to, do you?" Kim said shrewdly. "You know as well as I do that Steve Revellion wouldn't miss a few thousand dollars."

"Perhaps not, but he'd be furious if I walked off

with it," Carrie said. "He doesn't like a woman to get the better of him. In any case, I wouldn't do anything so dishonest. He'd get his own back somehow, that's certain. He's just so hard and mercenary you wouldn't believe it," she added, thinking of Janelle's story.

Kim looked at her in surprise. "But you like him, don't you? I mean, how could you help it, despite his being so—so tough? It would give me shivers all up and down my spine if I were engaged to him. I'll die of disappointment if you wriggle out of it, Carrie, honestly I will."

"Then it looks like you're going to die of disappointment," Carrie said lightly. She didn't feel inclined to tell Kim that it now appeared she had no choice in the matter. It seemed simpler to keep that to herself.

"If you don't marry him, then I'll owe you six thousand dollars," Kim said gloomily. "It will take me a lifetime to pay that off."

"You're immoral," Carrie said rather sharply. "You ran up those debts, Kim. Why should I marry a man I don't love because of that?"

"Oh, love," Kim shrugged. "I sometimes wonder what it's all about. Love wouldn't worry me if I had the chance of marrying a handsome millionaire. I'd be off to the church or the registry office or wherever like a shot. I'd soon learn to love him! In fact, I'd take Steve Revellion any time he asked me, marriage or not. I don't know what's the matter with you, Carrie. You're not still in love with Paul, are you?"

They had reached the flat, and Carrie didn't reply. She was beginning to realise that she wasn't still in love with Paul, but it was too soon to sort out her feelings properly.

"Well, *are* you?" Kim insisted as they went inside. But Carrie refused to discuss the matter.

"I'll work it out for myself, Kim. And I'd appreciate it if you don't keep telling me how nice it would be for you not to have to face up to that great big debt you incurred."

Kim looked hurt. "Carrie, you know I'm a—a compulsive spender. I just can't help myself, with *my* background."

"Then you'd better start helping it," Carrie said unsympathetically.

They took turns to shower, cooked dinner together, and afterwards watched television. There was just a hint of tension between them and Carrie found it hard to keep her mind on the drama they were watching. She couldn't help thinking that her life had really been turned upside down lately, thanks to Kim.

The play was still only half way through when Gene Lennox turned up, letting himself in with his own key and obviously taken aback to find someone else there with Kim. *It could have been those boys on the beach as well,* Carrie thought a little amused, so he was lucky. Kim, somewhat flustered, made the introductions, after remarking that she'd thought he was doing something else tonight. "This is my cousin, Carrie Adams. She's engaged to Steve Revellion."

Carrie smiled and said hello and Gene, a rather good-looking man with reddish hair and intelligent eyes, remarked, "So you're the girl who's making all the females round about gnash their teeth. One of them in particular, I believe! Somebody told me there'd been an announcement in the paper about coming nuptials. When's it to be?"

"We haven't got as far as thinking about that," Carrie said, very conscious from the way he was looking at her that he was wondering how on earth such an ordinary sort of girl had managed to hook so big a fish. He'd be really surprised if he knew of Kim's part in it, and possibly even more surprised if she told him that Janelle Lane was by no means gnashing her teeth, because she knew there weren't going to be any nuptials for Carrie Adams and Steve Revellion.

"If you're wise, you'll make it soon," Gene said. "Not count your chickens and all that. Steve Revellion has the reputation for being the hardest-to-hook man in the state."

Carrie smiled, but said nothing. Kim had switched off the television and was busily setting out glasses and drinks, but Carrie didn't sit down again or offer to help.

"It's really time I went," she told Kim, and was aware that Gene looked pleased. Kim protested, but only a little, and in a few minutes, Carrie was on her way downstairs.

She'd just reached the footpath when a car pulled up. It was Steve's Mercedes and her heart gave an unexpected lurch as she realised she had some readjusting to do. Things had changed radically since last time she'd seen Steve, which had been the previous night.

As he opened the car door and got out, she stepped forward to say brightly, "Hello! How did you know where to find me?"

He came to stand looking down at her in the light

of the street lamp, and she looked back at him, feeling herself tingle. Her mind was electrifyingly alive with her new knowledge of him, and she was aware that her actions, her tactics, were going to be different now that she understood their engagement was mere pretence that would last only as long as it took to bluff Janelle Lane into surrendering. And how long that would be, Carrie had no idea, but she didn't believe Steve would give way an inch.

"I didn't know where to find you," he said with a strange coldness. "For all I knew, you might have decided to take the plane to Sydney this afternoon."

"What? And leave all my beautiful new clothes behind?" she exclaimed widening her eyes. "Don't worry, I won't try to disappear." *Especially now that I know it's not necessary,* she added silently.

"If you do, you'll regret it," he said briefly. "Now get into the car. Let's not stand here all night." Then, when they were heading for home, he asked sharply, "Why didn't you tell somebody you were going to see Kim?"

Who?" she asked sceptically. "Janelle? Miss Higgins? I don't have to tell them how I choose to spend my time. Perhaps you'd better engage a private detective to spy on my movements, if you're all that interested."

"Don't be absurd," he said angrily. "You must have known very well I'd be concerned that you weren't there when I came back from Brisbane tonight."

She turned innocently wide dark eyes on him. "Honestly, Steve? I didn't know you cared," she said mockingly.

He shot her a sharp look. "You're very pert tonight."

"Am I? And you prefer me submissive, don't you, bowing to your divine will."

They'd reached the hotel now and she saw his frown of displeasure as he drove the car into the underground parking area. Each of them was silent as they took the lift to the fourteenth floor.

Janelle and her aunt were in the sitting room, Miss Higgins crocheting, Janelle reading a magazine and looking very beautiful in a long coral-coloured dress of pleated silk. She sent Carrie an artificial smile as she came into the room with Steve, who had put his arm possessively around her waist, his coldness and hostility discarded for Janelle's benefit, as Carrie well knew. She longed to escape from his embrace as Janelle's hard pale blue eyes looked her over.

"You've been out in the sun all day," Janelle observed and went on spitefully, "your nose is hideously red."

Carrie flushed angrily. Her face had caught the sun a little, but that was all. Steve pulled her closer. "It's a very charming little nose, Carrie," he commented and planted a light kiss on it to Carrie's discomfiture.

She drew away from him uneasily. "If you'll excuse me, I'll go to bed. I have a headache."

"Then run along," Steve said, not believing her to judge from the look in his blue eyes, but pretending tolerance and concern. "Would you like some aspirin?"

"I have some, thank you," she said quickly, and gasped as he took her in his arms, crushed her to him briefly, and kissed her lips. She fled the moment he released her. That had been entirely for Janelle's benefit, and she hated it. Oh, how she hated it—far more than she had done before Janelle clued her up.

It hadn't occurred to her that she'd be affected in quite this way by those revelations. Being kissed by Steve before had been bad enough, but now it was unbearable. It was something new to contend with, now that she didn't have to worry about marriage plans or feel guilty about not keeping her promise. Now she was sure that she was no more than an object that Steve was making use of for his own purely selfish purposes. It wasn't a pleasant sensation.

She'd reached the bedroom door when Steve said from behind her, "Carrie, there's something I have to say to you."

"What?" She turned and looked at him, her cheeks burning. *He had no right to be so handsome,* she thought, so handsome and so unfeeling, and she wondered briefly what she would most remember about this strange interlude in her life when it was over.

"I'm not saying it here," he said. "Go on in."

Reluctantly and with a faint shiver of apprehension, she obeyed him. Was he, by any chance, going to tell her the truth now? Reveal that this engagement was only a game after all? He followed her into the room and when she turned to face him he said forbiddingly, "You didn't put on much of a performance just now, by the way. I've told you what I expect."

"I know you have. And I know you're paying me six thousand dollars for it." She looked at him from the shelter of her long dark eyelashes and felt herself tremble. "I hate all this pretence," she burst out suddenly. "It makes me feel inhuman."

His blue eyes met hers glitteringly and his lip curled. "You hate pretence, do you? Then I suggest

we try a little realism and see how you like that."
With a sudden movement he kicked the door shut
and advanced on her, his expression so savage that
she backed away nervously. "I'll see if I can't
convince you we're not playing games, Carrie darling. Come here."

Her eyes widened and she took another step
backward. He followed her menacingly.

"Come here," he repeated, and when she raised
her arms involuntarily as if to protect herself, his
hands shot out to capture her wrists and in a moment
he had them fastened together behind her back with
the long steely fingers of one hand. Her back arched
as she struggled against him, and her breasts
strained against the material of her blue shirt.

"Let me go," she panted, but for an answer he put
his other hand low on her back and jerked her into
close and intimate contact with him. She could hear
his uneven breathing, feel the heat of his body and
the muscled hardness of his thighs, and in seconds
she knew that her closeness was rousing his passion.

"Is this pretence, Carrie?" he demanded, bending
his face toward her, his eyes searching hers almost
feverishly.

"No. Oh, no." It was all she managed to breathe
out before he set his mouth on hers and kissed her
with a brutality that shocked her. His heart was
pounding powerfully against the softness of her
breasts, and the next moment, she was swept up in
his arms and he was carrying her across the room,
his feet silent on the thick carpet. She was powerless
to prevent him as he thrust her onto the bed, pinning
her there with the weight of his muscular body, his
mouth still brusingly on hers while his fingers unfastened the buttons of her blouse.

"No!" she gasped again, freeing her mouth from his through sheer desperation.

"Why not?" he asked thickly. "You hate pretence, and nothing could be more real than this, could it?" He lowered his head to her breast and she felt the rasp of his chin against her tender skin. A shiver went through her and an intolerable weakness came over her limbs, a deep inertia invading her body so that for a long minute she lay passive as his lips caressed her. It wasn't until she felt his fingers at the waistband of her jeans that she roused from her torpor and began to struggle, her hands pushing him away from her with a strength she didn't know she possessed. Then somehow she'd escaped from him and was struggling to her feet, turning away from the bed as with trembling fingers she buttoned the front of her blouse. Her chest heaving, she heard him get up from the bed, and a quick fearful glance at him showed her that passion had darkened the blue of his eyes. She turned her head away, her nerves tingling.

"Leave me alone," she said, her voice husky and uncertain. She half expected him to pull her back into his arms and knew that if he did, there was no way to escape unless she screamed. Ludicrously, the very thought of having Janelle come to the door was more than enough to prevent her from doing that.

But he didn't touch her. He merely said mockingly, "So you don't believe in sex before marriage."

"No, I don't," she whispered, and as she spoke she remembered Janelle's hateful advice—If you haven't already seduced him, don't.

"Could it possibly be because there's another man in your life?" he said, and her lashes flew up.

"Who do you mean?"

"You know who I mean," he said, his nostrils

dilating. "You and your talk about pretence. You lied to me, didn't you, when you said you didn't have a boyfriend. Well you can forget him. Our engagement's public knowledge now. If *Paul* doesn't know about it yet, then he soon will."

Paul! Carrie swallowed convulsively, her face paling. "My letter! How did you get hold of it?"

"You were careless, Carrie. You dropped it somewhere and Nella picked it up. She handed it over to me for safekeeping when I came in tonight."

Nella? She might have guessed it. Carrie must have dropped it by the pool and Janelle had picked it up and of course she'd have read it, and decided that Steve must read it, too. She probably counted it as one more weakness in his position that Carrie turned out to have another boyfriend in the background. She'd been too cunning to give him the letter herself, so she'd handed the task over to her little chirruping aunt. And Steve had—

"And you read it," she exclaimed furiously. "My private correspondence! I think you're despicable." The blood had come back into her face and her cheeks were blazing.

"You can think what you like about me, Carrie," he said coolly. "Surely you know the old saying that all's fair in love and war."

"Yes, I do, but as far as you and I are concerned, love hardly comes into it."

"Then we'll have to assume it's war, won't we?" he said. "The eternal war of the sexes." He put his hand in his pocket and produced her letter, tossing it onto the dressing table. "I've revised my plans since reading that—which is what I wanted to talk to you about just now, before you brought up the little matter of pretence."

"Your plans?" she repeated haltingly. She had reached for the letter and was staring at her name on the envelope, in Paul's rather flamboyant writing. She looked up, her forehead creased. "Do you mean you've changed your plans about marrying me? That you—you don't want to go on with it?"

He made a cynical grimace. "Have I been acting, or talking, as if I don't want to go on with it? It's too bad for you, Carrie, but even apart from the fact I've handed over that cheque it doesn't suit me to free you now."

Not now, she thought. *Not until Janelle gives in—or you discover to your sorrow that you have to . . .* "So what are you going to do?" she stammered.

"I'm going to take you up to my hideout in the rain forest. You're going to be right out of the way when your boyfriend comes whizzing up here to work out something exciting with you and your legacy—whatever that means," he concluded explosively.

Carrie didn't attempt to enlighten him.

"If you object to that," he went on tightly, "then the alternative is that our marriage takes place in—let's see—I think I could arrange it for three days from now."

Carrie put up her head. She knew quite well he didn't intend marrying her at all, not in three days or in three years.

"Suppose I choose that?" she said, and had the satisfaction of seeing the surprised disbelief in his eyes.

"I don't think you will," he said, his eyes unreadable again. "And I'll admit that I agree with you that we should get to know each other better before we marry. A whole lot better, in fact. We can do that up in the rain forest."

Carrie's heart lurched. Get to know each other a whole lot better. Just what did that mean? Her glance went uncontrollably to the bed, its cover crumpled from where they'd lain together only minutes ago. Nervously, she checked the buttons of her blouse then pushed the tangle of dark hair back from her cheeks.

"How do you mean? Get to know each other better?"

"Well, how did *you* mean when you suggested it in the first place?" he drawled sardonically. "I'd say, in any way it can be achieved. Living together, eating and drinking together, talking, making love. It should all help. Marriage, in my view, should be for keeps. I don't believe in easy partings if they're at all avoidable."

Carrie was silent. They could learn everything there was to know about each other, but he still wouldn't marry her, for keeps or otherwise. She would have to watch her step. From what she'd already discovered about him, she didn't think he'd hesitate to get her to bed and then toss her out when it suited him, so long as they hadn't exchanged marriage vows. She sank down weakly on the arm of a chair, her mind in confusion. "Where is this hideout of yours?" she asked, her throat dry.

"Up on the plateau in the rain forest. I have a cabin there. It's not easy to find and it's not easy to get away from and I somehow don't think your boyfriend will make it that far. I still have some work to do, but we'll find enough time to get to know each other, I promise you. We'll leave in the morning. So before you go to bed, and whether you have a headache or not, you're to pack your things." He strode across the room and, flinging open the wardrobe, grabbed an armful of her clothes and threw them on the bed. "Get moving. You can pack now."

"Now?" Her eyes flashed angrily. "Who do you think you are to order me about like that? I really pity anyone who—" She stopped. Anyone who marries you, she'd been about to say. She started again. "How can you hope your marriage will last if you're so dictatorial? Women don't put up with that nowadays. You must be off your brain to think I'll—"

"Be quiet and do as you're told," he interrupted harshly. "I'm not going to engage in idiotic arguments with you."

"And I'm not going to obey idiotic orders," she retorted. "I'll pack my things how and when I choose. And *if* I choose. So get out of my room and try thinking of me as a person—an adult—instead of just some creature you can push around." In a moment, she was going to burst into tears, and she turned her back on him furiously and stood rigid, trying to control her inner trembling, and more than half expecting him to grab hold of her and shake her for her insolence.

But he didn't. After a few seconds he said in a cold controlled voice, "You'll want casual clothes, walking shoes, swimming gear. And something pretty for the evenings. But I'd prefer you to pack everything."

She said nothing, and a minute later she heard him go, closing the door behind him.

Carrie turned round slowly and looked first at the closed door, then at the things he'd tossed onto the bed, some of the expensive, lovely things he'd bought her in Brisbane. Still in her hand was Paul's letter, folded over and over by her nervous fingers. It was funny, really. He was taking her away to the rain forest so she wouldn't be there when Paul came. She hadn't wanted Paul to come, actually, though on consideration, she wondered if it might be at least a little less traumatic than being alone with Steve Revellion in some cabin in the rain forest—not easy to find, and not easy to get away from, but where he and she were going to get to know each other a whole lot better. Talking, eating, and making love. . . .

For a mad moment she thought of running away, leaving everything here, sneaking out after everyone had gone to bed. She tiptoed across the room to open the door and listen, and find out if they were still in the sitting room. But the door wouldn't open. The key was gone and Steve had actually locked her in. Carrie put her hands to her face. It was unbelievable that she, Carrie Adams, who'd spent the last three years of her life working for a Catering Supervisor's Certificate, saving her money assiduously, should now be locked in a bedroom by a millionaire who was using her to bring his mistress back into line.

And now she was expected to pack her bags and go away with him, alone, tomorrow.

It was all too much. Carrie hovered between weeping and laughing hysterically.

Perversely, she decided not to pack. She couldn't. She showered, got into her night things, the old garment that Kim had scoffed at as a relic of boarding school days. Then she went out onto the windy balcony to listen to the sea and to calm her nerves. The stars were bright in the night sky, foam decorated the darkness of the ocean and down below, around the hotel pool in the light of soft lamps where moths fluttered, a group of young people were fooling about enjoying themselves.

Carrie stood there for a long time and then she went inside and telephoned Kim. She could hear the phone ringing and ringing, and finally it was not Kim but Gene Lennox who answered, his voice cross. Carrie felt so embarrassed she almost hung up without speaking. Of course he was still there, and she'd probably interrupted their lovemaking.

"Who's there?" Gene repeated impatiently.

"It's Caroline Adams. Could I speak to Kim, please?"

"Now? Can't it wait till morning?"

"Not really."

"Then give me a message and I'll pass it on."

There was nothing else but to do as he asked. "Please tell Kim I'm going away in the morning to the rain forest. With Steve," she finished reluctantly.

"Oh. To his hideout," Gene said. Obviously he knew a great deal more about Steve than she did. "All right. I'll tell her. Good night, Carrie." He put down the receiver rather hurriedly and Carrie made a face. She'd wanted to talk to Kim, but it wouldn't really have made any difference.

She took up Paul's letter from the chest where she'd put it, and taking it from its envelope read it through thoughtfully. It had a decidedly proprietorial tone about it, she realised. "'You didn't lose much time going after that millionaire,'" she read, and she wondered what Steve had made of that. It had probably confirmed his belief that she had put Kim up to approaching him about a loan.

But how intolerably big-headed it was of Paul to

think she'd meekly come back into his arms after the cursory way he'd treated her!

With sudden decision, she sat down at the little writing desk to answer his letter.

Dear Paul,

Your letter was a complete surprise. I had the impression everything was cut and dried between you and Josie Tanner and I'd accepted it. I'm sorry your deal with her father didn't come off, but you can't come up here now. I can't explain it all, but strangely enough I have met my millionaire and I'm having a marvellous time, so you really did me a good turn the night you told me we were through. It's too late to go back now, but you have my good wishes and I'm sure something will work out for you as it has for me.

Carrie

Without rereading it, she put it in an envelope and addressed it. She could leave it at the reception desk in the morning to be posted, and even if it wasn't entirely truthful, it should at least stop Paul from rushing up to Queensland which was the last thing she wanted.

That done, she climbed into bed and put out the light.

In the darkness she could see an image of Steve Revellion's face floating above her—just as it had looked when she was lying here on this bed with him. She shivered as she relived the sensation of the touch of his lips on her breast, the pressure of his passionate male body on her unresisting femininity. He'd let her escape him. But supposing he hadn't? He could so easily have made love to her, seduced her. She'd thought of him as infinitely hard and ruthless, but he hadn't been as callous as that. In fact, she suspected that all he'd been doing was giving her a fright, to put a stop to her talk about pretence. Would it be different in his cabin in the rain forest? It made her shrink to think of tomorrow. She told herself that she hated him and yet, somewhere deep down, there was a sense of excitement at the thought of disappearing with him. She remembered Kim saying, "I'd go with him any time he asked me." But he hadn't asked Kim. He'd asked her, Caroline Adams.

No, that wasn't quite true, she corrected herself, turning restlessly on her back. He didn't really mean to marry her, or did he? She didn't know. Perhaps Janelle had been right. This was a game between Janelle Lane and Steve Revellion. Carrie didn't matter one iota. Except that having paid for it—and had he paid! Steve was going to use her any way he chose. Whether seducing her would be part of the deal she couldn't tell.

Anyhow, what could she do about it?

Soon it would all be over, and she'd be able to do whatever she liked. This interlude on the Gold Coast would all seem a dream.

Chapter Seven

They left early in the morning, but not so early that Janelle hadn't emerged from her room to see what was going on. Carrie had been awake since dawn, and had almost finished her packing when Steve knocked on her door and came in with a cup of tea and two slices of bread and butter, and the comment, "So you're up. Good! We'll leave as soon as you're ready."

She said nothing about the locked door, hoping he'd believe she hadn't been aware of it, and when finally she was ready and went in search of him, Janelle appeared, and wanted to know what was going on.

"I'm taking Carrie up to the rain forest for a while," Steve said carelessly, and Carrie saw the look of fury, quickly concealed, on the other girl's face.

"What on earth are you going to do up there, all

on your own?" she asked, her pale eyes as hard as stones.

Carrie's colour deepened as Steve's glance went to her and he said coolly, "I'll give you three guesses."

Janelle didn't guess, of course, but while Steve was arranging for the luggage to be taken down to the car, she told Carrie pityingly, "You're going to be bored to tears, so don't get all worked up imagining you're off to paradise. There's nothing and no one up there in the rain forest. Just two dreary people who live in a cabin and look after Steve's place and his garden. If he gets around to seducing you, it will only be from boredom." Carrie said nothing and Janelle's eyes sparkled angrily. "However, if it will give you a kick, don't think it will upset me. You're the one who'll be the casualty."

Steve returned then, so to Carrie's relief no more was said.

She left her letter at the reception desk though Kim was not yet there, and soon she and Steve were driving away from the coast and into the hinterland.

His hideout was certainly well tucked away. Up on the plateau, they followed the sealed road for some time. The view over to the coast was spectacular. The sea was a far off shimmering haze, and the tall towers of the high rise buildings of the Gold Coast shone like gold. Presently they left the good road and travelled along miles and miles of twisting gravel track, until at some point where Carrie hadn't even been aware there was a turn off, they took to wheel marks through bush so wild and primitive they seemed to be in another world.

Then unexpectedly at a turn in the bumpy rutted track that seemed to lead to nowhere, there was a gate, and beyond it a garden. Great hoop pines and bunya pines and burdekin plum trees shaded a well-kept lawn, while at one side of the garden, the earth dropped away into a valley thick with trees that looked utterly impenetrable. Carrie heard the weird call of the stockwhip birds as Steve pulled up in shade in front of a long log cabin. As they went onto the narrow verandah a man and woman came through the side garden to meet them—middle aged and respectfully friendly while Steve made the introductions.

"Jean and Alec Potter—my fiancée, Miss Carrie Adams. We're not going to bother you, so long as everything's in order."

Everything was in perfect order. The bedroom Steve showed Carrie to was scented with lavendar; and from the window Carrie saw the Potters disappearing in the direction of a thick grove of trees, and concluded they must have their own cabin there. Steve left her to settle in, and she unpacked her clothes quickly, hanging her dresses in a big hand-hewn wardrobe that was shiny with age and beautiful. Steve told her later it was made from red cedar—the "red gold" of the colony at one time, and one of the finest cabinet timbers in the world, but plundered by the early settlers and now extremely rare.

She was still unpacking when Steve came back to tell her, "You can do the housekeeping while we're here, Carrie—and the cooking. There are plenty of fresh vegetables in the garden, and you'll find meat and fish in the freezer."

Just as if we were married already, Carrie thought nervily. Well, she was no stranger to housework, and cooking for two would be child's play, but all the same she turned from hanging up the violet robe to say coolly, "Why should I cook for you, clean for you? I suppose you feel you're paying me for that."

"Not at all," he said icily. "I merely want to find out what sort of a girl you are. It's a bad start if you're not going to co-operate."

She flushed at the criticism. "I'll co-operate. But I didn't think my ability as a housekeeper would be of much interest to you."

His eyebrows rose. "You thought I was only interested in how you'd perform in bed?"

Taken aback, she blushed crimson. "I—I wasn't thinking of that. I merely meant you—you hardly need a wife who knows how to polish and cook and sweep."

"Well, I presume you can cook," he said. "But whether I need that kind of a wife or not doesn't matter. I'll be working for a few days myself, and I have rather old-fashioned ideas about idleness—and mischief."

"I can't imagine what kind of mischief I'd get into here," she retorted.

"There are limitations," he agreed dryly. "Which is one reason you're here. But without mischief, you might mope—hence, you're to be kept busy and forget your boyfriend, and keep it in mind that you and I have made an unwritten pact."

Which you have even less intention of keeping than I have, she thought as she turned away with a shrug.

She didn't really mind having to look after the cabin and prepare the meals. She was an expert cook because of her training, and it actually gave her pleasure during the next few days to surprise him with her skill and to find he really appreciated it. He spent most of the day working in a small study that opened off one end of the main room, and once Carrie had accepted the situation, she soon developed a routine. Housework took up part of the morning, arranging the flowers, watering the pot plants on the verandah. Then there was lunch to prepare, and at one o'clock Steve joined her, usually fairly abstracted and untalkative throughout the meal. More washing up, plans for dinner, and then she was free for a few hours. There was a swimming pool in the garden, but she was more interested in exploring the bush.

Dressed in old jeans and shirt, she ventured into the edge of the rain forest—a fantastic forest that awed as much as it fascinated her. She could hear various bird calls as she wandered down narrow paths, soft with decaying leaves and laced about by monkey vines and palm-like lawyer vines. High above in the canopy, the trees made a leafy green heaven so dense it took the place of the sky, and where the crazy looping of the vines turned it into a surrealistic dream world.

Each day, she followed the bird calls, but the birds were as elusive as will-o'-the-wisps. The only one she managed to observe was a large and beautiful bird that sat for a long time high up in a tree, uttering a loud cry over and over again. It's underside was purple and orange, and its bill pale red. She asked Steve about it at dinner that night and he told her it was a Wompoo pigeon, and promised to find her a book to read about the flora and fauna of the rain forest, if she were interested.

One evening after she'd finished the dishes, she discovered that for once he hadn't gone back to his study, but was still in the living room, leaning idly back in the sofa. She hesitated in the doorway, not knowing whether to join him or not. He seemed unaware of her presence, and for a long moment she stared at him taking in the curly black hair, the firm line of his cheek and jaw, the casual but good looking clothes he wore—a cinnamon shirt, light olive pants, so that he looked very much a man of the outdoors even though he'd spent the last few days at his desk.

After a moment he turned his head, and she caught with a shock, the brilliant blue of his eyes.

"What are you waiting for? Come and sit down and talk to me."

She crossed the room reluctantly, aware of his glance lingering on the chalk white lace-trimmed dress she'd chosen to wear, one of those he'd selected for her in Brisbane, in his undeniably knowledgeable way.

"I don't want to disturb you if you're still working on your papers," she said.

"For heaven's sake—do I look as if I'm working on my papers? I'm taking a break. Come and sit down here next to me," he added, indicating she sit on the sofa beside him.

"I thought you might be going over something in your mind," she said, obeying him but keeping as far away from him as she could when she sat down.

"Sure I'm going over something in my mind. I'm not just staring into space," he said, looking at her quizzically. "As a matter of fact, I've been thinking about you and your walks in the forest. For some reason, I imagined you read or rested in your room in the afternoons."

"I'm not old enough for that yet," she said dryly. "The forest's beautiful isn't it?"

"Do you think so?" He stretched a long arm

across the back of the settee, his jewel blue eyes assessing her.

"Those enormous trees," she said inadequately. "The long, long vines—and ferns growing up near the sky. I always hear a whole lot of birds, but the only one I've ever caught up with is that Wompoo pigeon."

"The others are probably the lyre birds," he said with a smile. "They're the most amazing mimics. But there are one or two things you should be wary of if you're going to venture into the rain forest. First and foremost, don't go too far or leave the path and lose yourself. I don't fancy the idea of going after you with a torch in the darkness when my dinner doesn't materialise."

"You needn't worry," she said quickly. "I have a great respect for that forest, and I wouldn't dream of getting lost when there's your dinner to cook."

He raised an eyebrow. "You're as thoughtful as a wife already," he said mockingly. "However, I was going to warn you to watch out for the stinging tree. Lovely pale green heart shaped leaves—I'm sure you'll find them entrancing. Maybe eight inches long and covered with tiny hairs, thousands of them, containing an acid that could have you in agony for hours."

"You're frightening me," she said. She'd seen those leaves, and thankfully, for some reason she hadn't touched them. "Would you prefer me to stay safely in the garden, doing nothing?"

"I'm not trying to spoil your fun," he said irritably. "I'm trying to educate you."

"Thank you. I'll watch my step. And if you'll let me have that book you mentioned, I'll start reading it and educate myself a little further. It will give me something to do while we're here."

"I've been neglecting you. Is that what you're implying?"

Carrie bit her lip. It was true a note of reproach had crept into her voice and now she was embarrassed. She had seen very little of him, and she hadn't been expecting that. She'd been expecting— *well, let's face it,* she thought, *a few love scenes.* Certainly not this business of spending almost the whole time by herself. Yet when there was no audience—no Janelle—where was the point in his making passes at her?

She said quickly, "It suits me perfectly well the way things are."

"Then it shouldn't," he said. "Considering that you've agreed to marry me. However, things will be different very shortly. I have to go across to the coast tomorrow, but after that we'll really get together."

Carrie digested that in silence. It occurred to her that he might have offered to take her with him, but perhaps he didn't want her in the way while he was sounding Janelle out. Or did he imagine Paul might be there? He wouldn't be. He'd have had her letter and would know that she didn't want him to come. Anyhow, she wasn't going to ask Steve to take her with him. She could amuse herself well here. All the same, she wondered if it would be all business or if most of his time would be spent with Janelle. She had curiously mixed feelings about that.

It seemed strange the next day when he wasn't there. He had left straight after breakfast, and

Carrie did the housework feeling oddly at a loss. She read some of the book he'd lent her, but it didn't hold her interest, and that afternoon she decided not to take her usual walk in the rain forest. Instead, she sat in the garden under the bunya pines, not even pretending to read but simply dreaming, letting her thoughts drift where they would. She thought of Steve, and wondered what he was doing at the coast. He was sure to see Janelle, and heaven knew what he'd let her believe had been happening up here at the cabin. She would certainly never believe they'd passed such an innocent few days. Carrie could hardly believe it herself. She'd been totally alone with Steve, and he hadn't even kissed her, hadn't once touched her. He might as well have been her brother. The seduction that could have happened through sheer boredom, according to Janelle, hadn't even shown any signs of taking place.

Carrie sat up suddenly. Anyone would think she was regretful about that, and she certainly wasn't. She wasn't in the least like Kim. She didn't relish the idea of having Steve Revellion take her to bed. It might have been different, she conceded, if—well, if she'd known there was no escape. If she'd had to accept that she must marry him, and that he wanted it. But he had plainly told her one woman would do as well as another.

Sickened by her thoughts, she went inside, got into her old yellow swim suit, and went out to the swimming pool. There she swam until she was exhausted, then lay on the soft grass on her face, mindless, limp. The sun wasn't nearly as burningly hot here as it was at the coast, but it was warm on her back, and soon she fell asleep.

She didn't hear the car when Steve came back. The first she knew of his return was when she came to and heard a splash, and starting up, dazed from her dreams, discovered that Steve had dived into the pool and was swimming as vigorously as she had done some time earlier. She flattened herself out again and watched him through half-closed eyes, ashamed of the way she was visually feasting on him, inwardly exulting that he was back.

It was loneliness, of course, she told herself, and only half believed it. He swam strongly, plainly regarding it as exercise, and then at last he emerged. She watched him through her lashes as, having climbed out of the pool, he stood on the narrow tile pressing the water from his streaming hair. Stripped, he was magnificent, his limbs muscular, his whole body tanned to mahogany against white swim shorts so minimal he could almost have been naked.

He was looking at her now, and she sat up as he walked across the grass to her.

"You're awake."

"Yes. And you're back. I—I didn't know when to expect you."

He was frowning at her as she curled her legs under her and looked up at him.

"Why are you wearing your old suit? I told you to get rid of your old clothes," he said, hands on his narrow hips.

Carrie felt herself bristle with antagonism. Her old clothes were not all that old, and she happened to be fond of this comfortable garment. A faint tinge of colour came into her cheeks as she told him almost haughtily, "I'm not used to taking orders about my habits of dress. As far as I'm concerned, what I wear for swimming is my own affair. There's no one around here to see me and think I'm not good enough for you, if that's what's on your mind."

It was hardly a submissive or friendly speech and she saw his nostrils dilate in anger.

"All that's beside the point," he grated out. "I've provided you with good clothes and you'll wear them. I don't care about the rest of the world. You're to please *me*—when I look at you I want you to look good."

"Do you really?" she snapped, equally angry. "I'm—I happen to be more than a clothes peg, Mr. Revellion. I'm a person, and I have personal tastes. I'm not mad about bikinis and—and having males of any kind look me over with—with predatory eyes." She scrambled to her feet. "I'm going inside to see about dinner, so you won't have to look at me any longer."

"Carry on," he said icily, but his eyes flashed blue fire.

She felt decidedly unhappy as she hurried away from him, and she was already regretting that she'd spoken to him the way she had. But then, he shouldn't have been so thoughtlessly rude to her. Perhaps he'd had no success in bringing Janelle to heel and was consequently in a bad mood. If that was it, then she didn't feel in the least sorry for him. Her own mood had been completely spoilt and it had been an oddly pleasant one. She hated herself now. One moment she'd been half in love with him, the next she was shouting at him like a fishwife. None of it added up to the Carrie Adams she was used to.

It had all blown over by dinner time. Or at any rate, both of them acted as if nothing had happened. Steve praised the meal, and she somehow made conversation and refrained from asking him how he'd spent the day and whether he'd seen Janelle. For his part, he offered her no information.

Afterward, they listened to music. He had a good collection of tapes, and having chosen the first one himself, he told Carrie to choose the next. She glanced through them quickly and then asked him, her eyes widened innocently, "Don't you have any disco music?"

"No, I don't," he said, leaning back in his chair, his eyes half-closed in the lamplight. "Is that what your taste runs to?"

It wasn't really, but somehow Carrie was feeling perverse. "Sometimes. It depends on my mood." She added deliberately, "But I suppose you're in the wrong age group to take an interest in disco."

He got to his feet. "Quite right. I'm too old for it and I haven't got time for it. But if it pleases you, ask Alec to bring something back from the coast for you tomorrow. If you insist, you can teach me about it. I admit my ignorance in that particular field. On the other hand, there are things I can teach you—things I'm *not* too old for."

"What?" she asked unwisely, and gasped as he seized her wrist and pulled her into his arms.

"This," he said against her mouth.

His kiss was burningly brief and she was free before she knew it. Her heart racing, she absorbed herself in choosing music from what was available.

He didn't touch her again after that, though her nerves were taut as she waited for something to happen. Instead, she went off to bed with a bewildering sense of frustration.

The next day was hot, and in the afternoon she decided to swim again—and to wear her yellow swimsuit. After all, Steve was working once more, so what did it matter? Besides, the bikinis he'd bought for her looked so tiny—revealed too much. Somehow she felt it would be immodest—it would be asking for trouble—to wear such sexy scraps. It would be different on the beach where all the girls were wearing this sort of thing, but here, with a possible, but not probable, audience of one, Carrie couldn't do it.

She was climbing out of the water when he came out to the pool at about five o'clock. He stood watching her until she'd fully emerged. She stood dripping on the tiles, shaking her hair back from her face. He strode towards her, then abruptly and shockingly took hold of the straps of her swimsuit and with one hard movement, stripped it off her. It was incredible. One moment she was decently clad, the next she was naked, her yellow swimsuit ignominiously around her ankles. With a little cry, she kicked the garment aside and ran for the cabin, tears of rage and mortification in her eyes.

"I told you not to wear that thing." His voice followed her harshly. "In the future, take notice of what I say."

She didn't go out again. Nothing on earth would have persuaded her. In her room, she flung herself on the bed and swore to herself that she wouldn't cook his dinner or do a lick of work for him from now on. She didn't care if they both starved or if the cabin looked like a slum. As for her clothes—she knew she wouldn't dare to wear anything from her old wardrobe. Not one thing. She didn't fancy being stripped naked again.

Presently she got up from the bed, wrapped herself in her robe, and went to the window. He was swimming. Arrogant, tyrannical man! And she was engaged to him. It didn't help to remind herself that it was all a sham. If she had romanticized the situation in his absence, she was back to reality now. Deliberately she blocked out of her mind his blazing blue eyes, the feel of his thick, curling hair in her fingers. He had said himself *one woman is as good as another*. She would never forget that.

Later on, she put on one of the lovely evening creations he had bought her in Brisbane; silky, black and gold with a gold camisole bodice. Far too dressy for a place like this, but if he wanted her to dress up for him then she would—with a vengeance. She looped her hair back from her cheeks and caught it at the side with tortoise shell clips, then made up her face elaborately, emphasising the darkness of her eyes with a subtle green eye shadow.

She hadn't done a thing about dinner, and she was defiant but more than a little scared as she sauntered into the living room and sat down, crossing one leg over the other—an action which revealed her slit skirt. Steve was pouring himself a Scotch and turned with the glass in his hand to glance at her and then to let his eyes take her in fully.

Instead of demanding why she wasn't getting his dinner—which was what she expected—he said, "You're looking exceptionally beautiful tonight, Carrie. Is it for my benefit?"

She flushed. "You could put it that way. I thought it was better to be safe than sorry."

"What's that supposed to mean?"

"That I don't like having my clothes torn off my back—just because they displease you."

With a twisted smile he said, "If it's any comfort

to you, you looked very pretty, Carrie—like a nymph in flight."

"It's no comfort to me at all," she said coldly, but her pulses were racing.

"Hmm. Do you want a drink?"

"I'll have some tonic water, please," she said stiffly.

"If that's what you fancy."

He brought her the drink then took one of the linen-covered chairs at an angle to hers and drank his Scotch, staring into space. The gas lamp flickered faintly, emphasizing the planes of his face and making his eyes gleam like blue fire. She watched him uneasily from under her long silky black lashes. What was he thinking as he downed his Scotch? And when was he going to say something about dinner? She sipped her tonic water and wished she'd asked for something different—a sherry, a Cinzano and ice. Anything that would give her a little confidence.

He looked up and met her eyes. "What are you thinking about, Carrie?"

Taken by surprise, she didn't know what to say, and parried, "Does it matter? What are *you* thinking about?"

"You," he said abruptly, and she reddened with shock. "Does that surprise you? It shouldn't, since we're living here like this. I think about you a great deal, and you're supposed to be thinking about me, too, you know. We have to learn about each other. That's why I want to know what's going on in your mind." He stood up and came to take her glass from her. "For all I know, you may spend your time thinking of someone else—Paul. Do you?"

Her eyes fell before his. Paul! What was Paul to her now? It was Steve who was in her mind, had been in it all day, and was there now, despite everything. But she wasn't going to give him the satisfaction of knowing that.

His fingers touched hers as he took her glass, and her nerves jumped. Her eyes flew guiltily to his. What had he read into that?

He turned away as if he'd noticed nothing. "I'll go across and ask Jean to get us something for dinner. Did you give that list to Alec by the way? Did he bring you back some disco tapes from the coast?"

"I didn't ask him," she said huskily. "It doesn't matter, anyhow." He had turned back to her and stood with his hands on his hips. He wore black polished cotton pants, a black shirt with a white unbuttoned collar, and he looked strikingly male. And strikingly arrogant. An odd little thrill ran along her nerves.

His eyes had moved to her hand and she discovered she was turning the diamond ring on her finger, turning and turning it. He looked back into her eyes and told her seriously, "If you like disco music, Carrie, then I want you to have it."

"I can live without it," she said ungraciously, and he frowned then turned away again and left the room.

She got up and wandered restlessly to the windows to look out into the darkness of the night. It was quiet here without the sound of the sea. The only noises were the moving of the trees in the night wind, the scufflings of creatures in the bush, and there was not a light to be seen except the stars in the sky. It was eerie, lonely, isolated. Yet the Potters' cabin was no more than a hundred yards away, hidden behind a clump of trees. She looked down at the ring on her finger. Would he insist on her keeping that when their engagement was over? It gave her a strange feeling. She didn't think she'd ever be able to wear it again, because it would remind her of him—of the blueness of his eyes as they stared into hers so unreadably, of the feel of his mouth against hers, of his hands moving on her body. . . .

She moved impatiently. She was becoming obsessed with the man. That was the result of being holed up here alone with him. It was the boredom Janelle had spoken of, and nothing else—but it could be dangerous. She began to wish she'd been sensible and hadn't put on this act—getting herself all dressed up and silently refusing to cook his dinner. Ordinarily, she'd have been busy and unassailable in the kitchen, but he could hardly have asked her to cook wearing this expensive get up. Abruptly, she went to the cabinet where the tapes were stored and selected a cassette without even bothering to see what it was. Anything, so long as when he came back there wouldn't be this silence that seemed to her to be saying things she didn't want to hear.

He was back in minutes, poured himself another Scotch, and without asking her, poured a sherry for Carrie.

She looked up as he handed it to her. "What did Mrs. Potter say?"

"She'll have something ready for us in thirty or forty minutes."

"Oh. But I meant, what—what did she think?"

He smiled crookedly. "I didn't ask. Probably that we've been making love and the time slipped away."

She blushed scarlet, and to hide her embarrassment, gulped down half her sherry.

He laughed. "Come on now, Carrie. Surely you know the Potters think we're lovers."

"I—I hadn't thought about it," she said jerkily. "But I suppose I'm not the first."

"Not the first *what?*"

"Not the first—mistress you've had here," she said, thinking of Janelle. She swallowed the rest of her drink and tried to appear unconcerned.

"But you're not my mistress, are you?" he said, and added, "Yet."

She flinched and her heart began to race. What a stupid thing for her to have said! But quite definitely she *wasn't* going to be his mistress. She put down her glass and said it aloud, her voice choked. "Being your mistress isn't—part of the arrangement."

He came over behind her chair and leaning down put his hands over her breasts, moving his fingers sensuously and rhythmically so that her heart seemed to come into her mouth and she felt herself tremble. He brought his face down close to hers, their cheeks touching. She could smell his after shave cologne and she heard the harsh sound of her own caught breath as his teeth bit her ear lobe sharply. She closed her eyes and he said softly, "A wife can be a mistress first, Carrie." Her heart pounding, she leaned back, letting him slide his hands inside her dress to lie warmly intimate against her bare breast.

"That's a mad thing to say," she said on a breath.

"Not so mad," he murmured, his voice thick with passion. Her senses were clamouring. His hands cupped her naked breasts, pressed against them urgently so that she felt sick with pleasure. Sick with desire, she realised when a moment later he drew

149

her out of the chair and turned her toward him. She was trembling and helpless. His arms closed around her and his mouth came down to hers, brushing across it tantalisingly. Her eyes were closed and she could hear the silence of the night, the beat of her heart, the beat of his. His hands slid gently down over her body, feeling the inward curve of her waist, reaching the smooth swell of her buttocks and resting there. She tasted honey on her lips and knew it was the taste of his mouth and she could feel herself warm and soft against him, aware of every nerve in his body, despite the clothes that separated them.

He kissed her till her breath was gone, and the urgency of his hands as they moved to the base of her spine communicated itself to her so that when he let her go, so they could both take a breath, she moaned feverishly, "Kiss me—kiss me. Don't let me go—"

As in a dream she felt herself lifted in his arms and carried through the lamplit room to the darkness of her bedroom and the softness of her bed. She lay with her eyes closed, her senses excruciatingly alive and demanding release—the release he could bring by loving her.

"Carrie, take your clothes off," he said softly, gently.

With a little gasp of shock she sat up, her eyes wide open. Moonlight came in through the wide window in a swathe across the bed and across his body. She could see the gleam of his naked torso, his shirt lying on the chair where he'd thrown it. His hands were at his belt and she—

She must be clean out of her mind. She went rigid, her eyes staring at him though his face was in shadow. He leaned towards her, one knee on the side of the bed and she gave a little cry and slid her feet to the floor, her one thought being to escape from him.

His hand shot out and he caught her roughly by the wrist, pulling her back, and taking no notice of her struggles.

What would have happened next she was never to know, because at that moment someone knocked loudly on the living room door, and Jean Potter's voice called, "Are you there, Mr. Revellion? I've brought your dinner."

Chapter Eight

Carrie didn't know what Steve felt, but her own highly pitched emotions were shattered, and she came back to reality with a sickening jolt. One of the tortoise shell clips had fallen from her hair and her cheeks felt hectic. Steve let go of her wrist and pushed past her in a huff to go to the door and shout, "Okay, Jean. Leave it on the table or wherever you like."

Carrie sank down on the bed. Oh, the shame of it! If Jean Potter thought they'd been making love half the afternoon, what must she think now, hearing Steve's ill-humoured voice coming from the bedroom? He had pushed the door wide open and a shaft of light came in from the living room lamps.

"Tidy yourself up," he told Carrie harshly, retrieving his shirt from where he'd flung it.

She waited till he'd left the room, then she put on the light and went to the mirror to look at her wide-eyed unsmiling reflection in the glass. She combed her hair, patched up her makeup and tidied her dress, which looked as if it had been pulled half off her and finally, with deep reluctance, went to join him. There was no way out of it, and strangely enough, she was actually hungry.

Jean had made them an omelette with a fresh mushroom filling. It reposed in a deep earthenware dish on the table, which she'd spread with a red-and-white checked cloth. She'd laid out knives and forks, and there were pats of butter and a plate of sliced homemade bread. A bottle of red wine and a platter of cheese completed the meal. Carrie sat down thankful for the softness of the light. She couldn't look at Steve and didn't want him to look at her, and deep down she knew why she felt so ashamed. She'd wanted him to make love to her. If she hadn't exactly led him on, then she hadn't rebuffed him. Understandably he'd thought he could go ahead and then she'd leaped away from him like the proverbial startled fawn.

He saw her seated and then busied himself opening the bottle of wine. The glasses filled, he sat down opposite her, looked across at her and exclaimed almost angrily, "For heaven's sake, can't you act like an adult? Do you have to assume the air of a—a schoolgirl who's been caught naked in front of the mirror?"

The blood rushed to her face, and she knew at that moment just how raw and inexperienced she must seem to him, and how she must irritate him. Well, what did it matter? She'd be out of his life soon enough, and he could go back to Janelle. She'd been his mistress for a long time, it wouldn't be boredom that drove him to her.

She let him help her to some of the omelette, sipped her wine, and in her mind turned over various things she could say, such as, *I'm sorry, I don't happen to be promiscuous and nearly losing my virginity is rather traumatic.* But she said nothing after all. She'd read somewhere that sometimes the best way to bring a situation back to normal was to say nothing, that talking too much could be an extra aggravation.

She ate her omelette, helped herself to bread and cheese, and finished her wine. And she didn't protest when he offered to make the coffee. When he brought it in from the kitchen, he asked her conversationally, "Were you and Paul lovers, Carrie?" Her nerves jumped. "No!" she exclaimed, over positively, and he raised his eyebrows skeptically.

"Was it his debt I paid off?"

"No," she said promptly.

"It was yours?"

She struggled with herself for a moment, and then lied. "Yes."

"I don't believe you," he said flatly. "I don't believe you're either a compulsive spender or a gambler."

"I can't help what you believe," she said. "Does it matter, anyhow? You've paid off the—my debts, and I've agreed to marry you. If that's what you want," she finished, her voice low.

He flashed her a hard look. "Are you trying to make yourself sound like a bought woman, in the hope that I'll take pity on you?" he asked cynically.

She shook her head, debating whether this was the moment to tell him she knew this was all a farce. Almost instantly she decided it wasn't. Since he was putting up the money, he had the right to play the game his way, and the wisest thing for her to do was to be quiet and simply let it all happen. By which she definitely didn't mean what had nearly happened a while ago in the bedroom. . . .

After they'd drunk their coffee, she took the dishes out to the kitchen and washed up. He didn't come to help her, but stayed in the living room, listening to some Greek music. When she'd finished, Carrie came to the door.

"I'm going to bed."

He looked across the room at her, his glance moving down from her shining dark hair to her bare shoulders, and the black and gold dress with its slit skirt. For a wild moment, she thought he was going to say, "I'm coming with you," but he didn't. He leaned back in his chair and said an indifferent, "Good night. Sleep well."

After that night, he didn't even try to make love to her. But during the next few days, while he spent his mornings in the study, he devoted himself largely to her during the rest of the day. They swam together in the pool, and although Carrie obediently wore the bikinis he'd bought her on the Gold Coast, he made no comment and his eyes never lingered on her figure for more than a moment. In fact, he seemed quite indifferent to her physically, and she found it oddly disturbing.

On several occasions they took walks into the rain forest, and she was gratified to discover that reading the book he had given her enabled her to take an intelligent interest in the things he pointed out to her—the birds nest ferns high up in the trees, the elkhorns, the beautiful orange blossom orchids. She was able to recognise for herself the strangler figs with their great network of aerial roots that gradu-

ally fused together and killed the tree in whose
branches the fig had started its life. She marvelled at
the rope-like loops of the monkey vines, tangled
together high in the trees. She had read that many of
these vines were hundreds of years old and were
carried upwards by the trees to which they clung.
Sometimes there were heavy tropical storms late in
the afternoon, and then the forest was both eerie
and fascinating, mysteriously dark and full of bird
calls and the dripping of water from tree and fern.

At night, they listened to music or talked—about
art, politics, religion, dreams, and though she found
their conversations stimulating, Carrie couldn't be
happy. She wanted him to make love to her and she
couldn't hide the fact from herself as she lay restless
and wakeful in bed at night. It was just as though she
had become infatuated with him. Which, she finally
admitted to herself, she had. It was a disturbing
admission, because she knew, thanks to Janelle's
revelations, that it was all leading nowhere. She
supposed she should be grateful to Janelle, otherwise heaven knew how far she'd have let her feelings
lead her.

She was learning how much Quaama Springs
meant to him, which added strength to what Janelle
had told her. He'd talked about the cattle station
several times at night, and even apart from what he
said, Carrie could tell by the tone of his voice how
deep his affection for it was.

All in all, she thought, her eyes wide in the
darkness of her room, *she should be thankful he was
leaving her alone.* She didn't want him to seduce her
out of boredom, and then forsake her, as he was
going to forsake her. She remembered he'd asked if

she and Paul had been lovers, and it occurred to her that he could be taking pity on her because she was a virgin. Her thoughts exhausted her and yet she couldn't sleep, and it didn't seem to help when she told herself that what she felt was no more than infatuation, that she'd recover from it in a flash once she was away from here, away from him. Deep down, she knew very well she didn't want it all to end. She knew she wanted this truce that he seemed to have called to end in his making love to her, in her own capitulation. Yet where was the sense in that? It wasn't going to alter the facts.

In the morning, over breakfast, he told her abstractedly, "I'm going down to the coast for a couple of days, Carrie."

A couple of days! She felt her spirits go down with a thud.

"I have some business to see to," he explained. He poured himself a second cup of coffee, and Carrie watched him covertly, her eyes lingering on his newly shaven jaw, on the line where his lips met—a hard masculine line, yet with that enigmatic and unreadable upwards quirk at its ends.

She could guess well enough what his business was, and she asked, looking up at him, "Are Janelle and Miss Higgins still staying in your apartment, Steve?"

He flashed her a blue glance. "How should I know?" he snapped.

She lowered her eyes, rebuffed. *He's edgy,* she thought. *And he does know.* Of course Janelle was still there—waiting for him to agree to what she wanted, or waiting to give in, just so long as he'd give Carrie her marching orders.

"Could I come with you, Steve?" she murmured, not very hopefully.

"No. You can wait here," he told her emphatically. "I'll be back in a couple of days. I won't have time to be squiring you around, I have too much to accomplish. You're not by any chance hankering to find out if your friend Paul is around? Because if he is, then he's going to find out that you're not available, and hence that there's nothing doing as far as you're concerned."

"I could tell him *that* myself," she said, her cheeks tinged with colour.

"I wouldn't trust you," he said, his voice hard.

"You don't trust anyone, do you?" she flared.

"That's right. And women least of all," he agreed and got up from the table.

At that moment, she hated him. He wanted everything his own way. Suppose she had still been in love with Paul, what right had he to come between them, under the circumstances? It wasn't as if *he* wanted her. The thought of staying here on her own was unbearable. She'd rather go with him, know what was happening, be told on the spot that it was all over, instead of waiting here, uncertain of the fate of her future.

"As it happens, I wrote and told Paul not to come," she said after a moment.

He smiled cynically. "He'll still come, Carrie. Don't underestimate your own charms."

Her charms! *He* had no trouble resisting them.

He left ten minutes later with no more than a word of goodbye. Once the sound of the car had gone, she felt utterly lost. She wanted him back—*warts and all,* she thought wryly, and in that moment she admitted she was incurably addicted to him. Was it love? She hadn't enough experience to know. She'd once thought she was in love with Paul, and had found very quickly that she was not.

She went inside to clear up the breakfast things and tidy the house. In his room, she stripped the sheets from the bed and replaced them with fresh linen. She caught the lingering scent of his cologne and found he'd left the bottle unstoppered. She dabbed some on her wrist and felt the sick nostalgia that evocative perfumes can arouse. He hadn't taken his brushes with him and she picked one up and examined it lovingly. Silver backed, old-fashioned, with his initials engraved on it. A.S.R. Did the A stand for Anthony, after his father? As she finished making the bed, replacing the pillows and smoothing the bedspread, she reflected that he must sleep naked. She'd never seen any pyjamas lying around.

A little alarmed at the path her thoughts were taking, she left the room quickly and went into the garden to water and cut some flowers. The two empty days ahead of her without him seemed to stretch on endlessly.

Yet somehow, the time passed, the day went by. She ate alone, swam alone, walked alone in the rain forest, then hurried back as the light began to go, to eat a lonely meal, to play some music, to pretend to read a book. But all the time she was thinking of him, wondering what was happening over at the coast, and staring vacantly across the room at the wide windows that looked out into darkness. She didn't think she'd be able to sleep.

When she finally decided to go to bed, she went to his room and lay on his bed, and admitted openly to herself what was the matter with her. She was not just addicted to him. She was *in love* with him.

She cried herself to sleep.

She woke to another day and the moment she was conscious her mind was full of him. Love, she discovered, was like a sickness. You were helpless. There was nothing you could do about it. She showered, dressed, made coffee and brooded. In the garden, she paced up and down under the great pines. Tomorrow he'd be back. She both longed for it and dreaded it, because of what he might have to say to her. "Pack!" He'd ordered her to pack once before and she'd defied him. Defiance was going to be no use this time. She'd made a promise to him with the full intention of breaking it, and now all she wanted was to be forced to keep it. Otherwise, what was there in life?

She flung herself on the grass by the swimming pool and went to sleep.

The sound of a motor woke her, and she sat up feeling confused. Steve! What day was it? He wasn't due back till tomorrow.

But it wasn't Steve. Paul Stanhope emerged from the car that had pulled up on the drive. Carrie stared at him as though he were a ghost. That arrogant face, the perfectly groomed hair . . . The smiling, confident manner as he came toward her . . . they were all so empty now.

"Carrie!" he exclaimed, and the look in his greenish eyes was wary as if he were far from sure of his reception.

Carrie scrambled to her feet and tried to smile. "Paul! How on earth did you find your way here?"

He grinned more confidently, but he didn't try to

kiss her. "I followed instructions, though I'll admit I was somewhat doubtful when that track seemed to lead nowhere but into the jungle. Still, here I am. Are you glad to see me, Carrie?"

No, she wasn't. And she wished that she were. It would be such a relief to have found she was in love with him after all. Instead of answering him, she smiled again and asked, "Have you had lunch?"

"Lunch?" he repeated. "For heavens sake, it's three o'clock or thereabouts! But I could do with a cold drink. I'm absolutely parched." He glanced toward the cabin. "I suppose there's someone around who'll bring a tray of drinks, if you clap your hands?"

"I'm afraid not," she said flushing. "But come inside, there's plenty of fruit juice in the fridge."

He didn't sit down in the living room when she suggested it, but followed her out to the kitchen and looked around it curiously.

"It's adequate, I suppose," he commented while she found a tray and glasses, poured juice into a tall glass jug. "Not exactly what I'd have expected. I thought even in the wilds, a millionaire would have a super set-up."

He paused, and Carrie wondered what he was thinking, what conclusions he'd drawn about her being here alone with Steve. And who had told him how to get here. Steve? Surely not. Yet if he and Janelle had resolved their differences, why not? Her heart went cold. In the midst of putting biscuits on the tray—because she hadn't eaten since her meagre breakfast—she suddenly felt sick. That must be it. She let him carry the tray out to the table in the garden, and asked, trying to sound casual, "Did you meet Steve, Paul?"

"No, I didn't. I heard he was at the coast though, so I knew I wasn't going to burst in on anything here." He set the tray down on the table in the shade of the pines and Carrie sat down and helped herself to a biscuit. So Steve hadn't sent him, the world hadn't come to an end—yet.

"You shouldn't have come, Paul," she said. "I–I told you not to."

"I know you did. But I wanted to find out exactly what was going on." His greenish eyes were examining her face minutely, as if they were looking for something—Carrie didn't know exactly what. Some change in her, perhaps. She turned her face aside and bit her lip. "I had a suspicion you might be paying me back in kind for Josie Tanner, as a matter of fact, with all that stuff about a millionaire. I thought you'd probably got yourself some work up here. Anyhow, Kim told me differently." He reached out for her left hand and a look at her diamond ring. "So he's practically a millionaire, is he?"

Carrie moved her shoulders uncomfortably. "Does it matter all that much what he is?"

Paul smiled knowingly. "It could explain a lot. What kind of a guy is he? Old enough to be your father, I suppose."

"Not really," Carrie said carefully. She didn't want to talk to Paul about Steve. She took another biscuit and looked away from him, across at the swimming pool, glittering under the blue sky.

"Well, anyhow, I have a message for you, Carrie," Paul said, his tone altering subtly so that for some reason her heart began to thud.

"What do you mean? Who's it from?" she asked, turning back to him swiftly.

"An old duck called Miss Higgins," he said. "She wants you to know that Steve Revellion won't be coming back here tomorrow after all. She said to tell you that he and Mrs. Lane—whoever she might be—have had a long talk. She seemed to think you'd know what she was talking about."

Yes. Of course she knew what Miss Higgins was talking about. Carrie set her glass down on the table, because her hand was shaking too much to hold it. The colour had drained from her face and she looked at Paul without seeing him. *So it had happened. They'd talked—one of them had given in. Janelle,* she thought. *And Carrie Adams' day was over. He just wasn't coming back. Oh, how callous, how cruel,* her heart cried. *Yet it wasn't really like that. There'd never been anything real between them. There'd been no words of love. If he'd almost seduced her it had been through boredom—or through habit,* she told herself cynically. And those last few days—he'd been on his guard, and he hadn't even touched her. She really had nothing to complain about. And this was what she'd wanted. Once. In another life.

Paul said into the confusion of her emotions, "It sounds as if you're getting the push, Carrie. Not surprising, really. You're taking quite a chance when you take up with a man you hardly know. Besides, you're hardly millionaire material."

That was true, but it hurt all the same. He hadn't needed to say that. As for her taking up with a man she hardly knew, she couldn't explain that to him. It was Kim's story.

"It's just as well I came to look you up, isn't it?" Paul went on. "And listen, Carrie. I want you to believe this. I never felt about Josie the way I feel about you. What's more, I refuse to believe you

163

could feel more for this Revellion guy, however rich he is, than you feel for me. We've known each other three years. And how long have you known him?"

Forever, Carrie thought insanely, even though she knew that at this moment, he'd probably all but forgotten her. You don't have any compunction in dropping a girl who owes you six thousand dollars. You simply say, *Forget it. Go in peace.* And she goes.

Carrie heard her own slightly hysterical laugh, and tried to get herself in hand. But she wished, oh how she wished, that Paul would go away. She wanted badly to be alone, to lick her wounds, to assimilate what had happened. Somewhere away at the back of her mind she didn't trust that message Paul had brought from Nella Higgins. She couldn't help remembering that Janelle had used Nella once before, to hand over that letter to Steve. Mightn't the same sort of thing have happened again? Wasn't it possible Janelle had told Nella to give this message to Paul so as to get rid of Carrie?

Completely ignoring Paul's question, she asked him, "How did you come to meet Miss Higgins, Paul?"

"Through Kim," he said promptly. "She kept asking Kim if I'd arrived, because of this message she had for me."

"What did Kim tell you?" Carrie asked.

"About what?"

"About me and Steve."

He shrugged. "She was a bit mysterious about it all. She didn't say much except that you were engaged to him. I got the impression she didn't want to talk about it. She's got herself engaged, too, by the way, to a guy called Gene. She asked me to tell you. They're planning to be married in a month or so, and I think she was more interested in that than in anything else."

"Well, that's great," Carrie said tiredly. "I'm really pleased. I expect she'll give up her job at the hotel any time now."

"I wouldn't know about that," Paul said. "Anyhow, Carrie, now that you know your millionaire's deserted you—how about coming back home with me?"

Carrie said no without even thinking. Paul looked at her sharply, his green eyes surly. "Do you want me to grovel, to go down on my knees? I admit I made a mistake. I got carried away by the thought of running my own restaurant. But I'm not seeing Josie anymore. We're all washed up. She won't take a step without her father's approval, and now he knows the extent of my finances he doesn't approve of me and that's that. I was crazy ever to be bothered with her. Is that what you want to hear? I mean it, Carrie. All I really want is for you and me to get together and start building our future."

"Please, Paul," she interrupted, unsure whether he was talking about their personal relationship or the catering business, but not wanting to be involved with him either way. "It's just not possible—"

"Of course it's possible," he retorted. "Your millionaire boyfriend, from what I've gathered, couldn't care less what you do. As for you and me, we've both stepped out of line for a bit, but it doesn't have to ruin our lives and all the plans we made before it happened. I don't pretend to know exactly what you've been up to, but I do know your idyll has come to an end." He flicked a look at the cabin and then grimaced, as his eyes came back to Carrie. "I won't ask you any questions, Carrie. I won't even ask you what went on when you and Steve Revellion were sharing that cabin."

Carrie's colour rose. "You can ask all you like. Nothing went on, whether you believe it or not."

He shrugged. "Well, you still have your virginal look—but it's a fact you're a lot sexier somehow than you used to be. And I'm still crazy about you, Carrie. So why don't we just start over again, right at the beginning? Come back to Sydney with me and we'll make it a business relationship for a start, and see how we go from there. I do have a little money, and you'll have that legacy from your aunt, and if we pool it, it will give us a good start."

Carrie drew a deep breath. "Paul, I don't have that money any longer. I wasn't going to tell you because it didn't seem necessary, but now I suppose I must."

He looked at her suspiciously. "What do you mean? You always said it would just fall into your lap when you turned twenty-one."

"Yes, I know. But, well, I've promised it to–to someone who's got into debt. I won't have a cent."

He was staring at her suspiciously. "Someone? Who?" He reached for the jug of fruit juice and poured himself another glassful. "Are you trying to put me off, Carrie?"

"No." she said, though it was only half true.

Paul's eyes narrowed. He took a long drink, then set his glass down. "It's Kim, is it?" She didn't deny it and he went on angrily, "And you're just lying down and letting her walk over you, are you? We need that money, Carrie. You're not responsible for her debts. When's she going to pay it off? And what's it for? Surely she can go without it. You tell her it's all off. This man she's going to marry can take it over if he's so keen on her."

"Just don't try to organise everyone," Carrie said. "My arrangements with Kim are my own business. All you need to know is that I don't have any capital to invest, and nothing you say is going to change it."

He made an ugly grimace. His eyes had grown hostile, but Carrie met them steadily. She'd learned something from telling him that lie—though for all she knew, it could very well be true. She had no way of knowing how things were going to work out for her financially.

"You've changed, Carrie," he said. "And not for the better. I always thought of you as a steady sensible sort of girl, but now you seem to have run right off the tracks—rushing from one mad venture to another. I'd say you're all set to ruin your life."

"Perhaps that's how it seems to you, Paul," she said quietly. Right at this moment she was inclined to agree with him. Her life, in fact, seemed already to be in ruins. "But you're quite right, I have changed, and you'll have to believe that I don't want to tie myself up to you in any way at all. You really shouldn't have come up here. I told you not to."

He uttered an impatient exclamation. "For heavens sake—I couldn't just swallow down that vague story about a millionaire and the great time you were having. Quite frankly, I think you're off your head. What did you do? Promise the money to Kim because you really believed some wealthy guy you'd barely met was going to marry you and set you up for the rest of your life? It's obvious even to me he's just been playing around with you and now he's dropped you for somebody else. You could probably get something out of him still, if you were that sort of girl—and maybe you are that sort of girl, I wouldn't know." He got to his feet abruptly. "Well, it looks like I've wasted my time and money coming up here to see you. But if you want a lift over to the coast, I'll wait around while you pack up."

Carrie shook her head. "No, thank you, Paul. I'll work things out my own way."

"I don't reckon you're going to have your own way, Carrie," he said with a shrug. "Why don't you get out while you have the chance? He's not coming back."

"I'll manage," she said, though in her heart she was far from certain of that.

"Then do as you please," he said angrily and moved towards his car. "I'll probably go straight up to Brisbane and take the plane home from there. I can turn this car in at the airport." He hesitated as if he still expected her to change her mind, but she let him go without saying anything else, other than good-bye. She had the terrible feeling that she was going to burst into tears at any moment, and all she wanted was for him to disappear. And then, as he drove off, she had a mad impulse to run after him and ask him to wait, to take her with him. Because, wouldn't it be better to go now, instead of staying here, waiting, hoping? All the same, that was what she was going to do.

She didn't run after him and she didn't burst into tears. She turned away and went slowly into the cabin to her bedroom. There she lay face down on the bed and told herself fiercely that she didn't believe that message from Nella Higgins. It was just a plot of Janelle's so that she'd disappear with Paul and never see Steve again. Of course, if he didn't turn up tomorrow, then she would know it had been true. Not that it made any difference in the long run, because if he did come back, it would only be to tell her that he was releasing her from her promise, that he was going to marry Janelle after all. She'd have given in, Carrie was sure of it. She wanted Steve, and all he had, far too much to hold out for long.

She really should have gone with Paul. It would have been so much easier.

She got up from the bed and went out to the kitchen. She'd do some cooking. That would keep her from thinking. She'd bake a cake, make a casserole . . . Then if he came tomorrow—

It still wouldn't make any difference. What was the use of pretending? *And what was the use of tears?* she asked herself angrily, brushing them away from her eyes.

Chapter Nine

She wakened in the night to thunder and the sound of heavy rain. It was a sound she'd loved all her life. Even in Sydney, the rain could be torrential, here it was almost tropical in its intensity as it pounded on the roof. But she didn't love it now. It had disturbed her rest and she couldn't get back to sleep for a long time, thinking about Steve, wondering if she'd ever see him again.

In the morning, it was still raining and heavy grey clouds swarmed across the sky. The air was heavy and humid. Carrie tried to decide what time she could begin to watch out for Steve, if indeed he were coming, but she had absolutely nothing to base her calculations on. All the same, she was convinced he'd arrive some time. He wouldn't just leave her to wait and to worry when he'd told her he'd be back today. He'd come, even if it was only to tell her to pack her bags, before he took her back to the coast and said good-bye forever.

The day passed and he didn't come and her imagination ran riot. Janelle had given in—he was so elated he'd completely forgotten about Carrie Adams, alone in his cabin in the rain forest. It mattered nothing to him how she coped. She wandered dementedly back and forth on the lawn by the swimming pool. The rain had temporarily ceased, but the air was so hot her nerves were at screaming point. Was she to wait here until he remembered her and sent someone to fetch her? Or should she go over to the Potters' cabin and ask them to rescue her, to take her back to civilisation? She shrank from the thought, especially since she knew they believed she and Steve were lovers.

Oh, how she wished she'd vanished with Paul when she had the chance! Steve was the most callous man she'd ever encountered, and she hated him with every fibre of her being. Yet even as she told herself that, she knew very well that if he should drive up now, if she could raise her eyes and see him climbing out of his car, her nerves would at once be on fire and she'd be under his spell again.

Quite simply, she was in love with him. Madly, dementedly, helplessly. And hopelessly . . .

Later in the afternoon, unable to relax, certain now that he wasn't coming and that Nella Higgins had told Paul the truth, she set out for a walk in the rain forest.

Mouth set, eyes brooding, she followed the narrow rain-sodden path, intent on not tripping over the coiled monkey vines that were like traps across the way. Frogs croaked, birds called, and now and again big drops of water fell on her head. She was lightly dressed in cotton shorts and shirt, but soon her clothes were wet with perspiration. It was steamy and airless amongst the tropical growth, after all the rain. The deep need for distraction made her listen intently to the calls of birds that came from all around her. She knew well enough by now that they were lyre birds, prankish and elusive mimics that always managed to keep just out of sight. Carrie began to follow the sounds, telling herself, "If I catch a glimpse of that bird it means Steve will come and everything will be all right."

It was a long and fruitless game. Now and again she stood quite still, listening intently, and then moved silently and cautiously forward. But however long she waited, and however quietly she moved, she never caught sight of a single bird. Her spirits sagged and she grew desperate, wishing she hadn't persuaded herself that success meant Steve would come. It didn't mean a thing, and by now she knew he wasn't coming. Catching a glimpse of a lyre bird wasn't going to change anything.

It wasn't until thunder rolled overhead that she realised she hadn't the least idea where she was. She'd wandered on and on amongst the trees, forgetting the path, and in this forest everything looked the same. There was nothing to see but the great buttresses of trees, the looping twisting vines, the elkhorns and orchids perched high in the branches, picturesque against the green canopy. No wonder Steve had warned her always to stick to the path. She had always done so meticulously until today, and now as she stood staring about her, she hadn't the faintest idea whether she was facing north, south, east or west, of if she were a mile or a hundred yards from the cabin. She could not see the sky, but the thickening gloom and the repeated rolls of thunder told her that a big storm was coming and she felt the stirring of fear in her heart.

Before she knew what she was doing she'd begun to run, purposelessly, directionlessly, dodging trees, tripping over roots and buttresses and vines. Thunder vibrated overhead, so loud and so close that she clapped her hands over her ears and cowered against the netted aerial roots of a great strangler fig. Rain began to fall in sheets. In seconds she was drenched; the water ran down into her eyes from her soaked and flattened hair.

She stood still, trying to control her breathing and her fear. High above, the wind had begun to blow the tops of the trees so that they swayed violently. The movement was hypnotic and terrifying. Staring upwards, Carrie had the feeling that the whole forest was about to crash down on top of her. Unable to help herself, she screamed aloud, and the sound of her own voice made her heart race. As though she couldn't stop, she screamed again and again, repeating Steve's name over and over, each time more loudly than the last.

"Steve! *Steve!* STEVE!"

But it was no use screaming. No one would hear her, and at last she was quiet, and biting hard on her lower lip to stop its trembling. The rain forest had grown ominously dark. Great drops of rain were still pelting down. All around was a mad tangle of vines that writhed across the ground like monstrous snakes and made grotesque prisoners of the trees. Carrie felt deep in her bones that she was where no man had ever been—and where no man would ever come. She was lost to the world forever.

Suddenly, a streak of fire jetted down through the trees and immediately after the thunder clamoured. Carrie felt goose pimples prickle all over her skin. She pressed back against the tree, hearing the creaking and groaning of a hundred branches above her, lashed by the wind and the rain. And then, through the racket that nature was making, she thought she heard a human voice. Was it an answer to her shrieks of a few moments ago, or was she imagining it?

"Carrie!"

It was Steve! She was sure of it. Her heart leaping, she began to run, panting, as she gasped out his name. She heard him call again, and changed direction, running clumsily and desperately in the direction of the voice, praying it wouldn't be as elusive as the bird calls she'd followed so futilely earlier on.

Then her heart seemed to stop. There was a crushing sound from above and behind her, and with the crackling of a thousand fireworks, a great branch hurtled through the air and fell no more than inches from her. With a feeling of dread, she knew a tree was falling but she dared not look back. Careless with panic, she caught her foot in a vine and felt a spasm of excruciating pain in her ankle as she fell. The breath was knocked out of her as her body hit the ground. She felt the earth vibrate as a huge tree, having smashed and blundered its way down through the forest, finally met the ground. The shock of it jolted through her body so violently she thought she'd been struck. But her heart was still beating and she could hear the blood pounding in her ears.

For a long moment she stayed where she was, petrified. *Get up,* she kept repeating to herself. *Prove that you're still alive.*

But she still hadn't managed to move when Steve's voice said close to her ear, "Carrie! Oh, heavens—Carrie—speak to me for pity's sake—"

She felt his hand on her shoulder as he moved her gently, and she stared up into his face and saw the pallor under his tanned skin, the deep lines from his nostrils to the corners of his mouth. His eyes were like blue lightning and water dripped from his curling black hair. Still half-stunned, Carrie thought she'd never known a deeper happiness in her life than simply to have him there, looking down at her. She tried to say something, but the only sound she uttered was a sob, and as she struggled to sit up his arms enfolded her tenderly and he said almost inaudibly, "I thought you'd been killed for sure."

Her eyes went to the great tree stretched out on the ground amongst a ruin of broken branches. It was a strangler fig, surely the very tree against which she'd pressed herself so trustingly only minutes before. Overhead, a mass of broken vines dangled, still twitching, and she shuddered to think what would have happened to her if Steve hadn't called her name when he had, if she hadn't followed the sound of his voice.

"Oh, Steve, Steve," she muttered, leaning against him. "I knew you'd come—I knew you wouldn't leave me." Insane meaningless words, but held here against the warmth of his body she felt safer than she'd ever felt in her life. "I got lost," she murmured. "Following those stupid lyre birds."

She didn't think he heard what she was mumbling about, but he held her a little away from him, his eyes running quickly over her sodden form, the clinging shirt, the brief shorts, both of them filthy now. She pushed the wet hair back from her face, feeling an odd contentment that was completely irrational but that she couldn't control.

"How did you find me?"

"By a freakish chance I happened to be around. And I heard you shouting." He smiled crookedly.

"If you hadn't called me, I might have been killed."

"You nearly were," he said grimly. "When I saw you lying there I thought—" He stopped, a nerve jerking in his jaw. "Come on, Carrie. I'd better get you home. Are you all right?"

She nodded, and it wasn't till she tried to get to her feet that she remembered she'd wrenched her ankle when she'd tripped in the vine, and her face contorted with pain.

"Oh, my ankle!" she exclaimed clutching at him. "I twisted it when I fell. It—it will be all right in a minute."

But it wasn't all right. As soon as she put her weight on it she all but passed out, closing her eyes in agony, feeling sweat break out on her skin. A moment later, he'd swung her up in his arms and begun to carry her through the rain that still came down in big drops through the trees.

Recovering a little she protested. "You can't carry me all that way, Steve. Let me down—if I can just lean on you—"

"Keep still," he said, walking on. "It's not far."

"But it must be—I came a long way."

"Then you've been walking in a circle."

She didn't altogether believe him, but she gave in, relaxing in his arms. She felt the strength of his muscles, and the rhythmic movement as he walked steadily on through the rain lulled her.

It seemed not very much later that they emerged from the forest and reached his hideout. Across the lawn, dramatically golden-green in a sudden burst of late sunlight that found its way through the dark purplish grey clouds and the big bright drops of the rain, was the cabin. Home! Carrie feasted her eyes on it hungrily and then blinked. There was no car on the drive. So how had he come?

"Where's your car?" she asked bewilderedly.

"About fifteen kilometers back along the road," he said. "I couldn't get through. There's been a rockfall and half the road has given way and collapsed into the gully. I took a short cut and walked through the rain forest—which is how I came to find you." He carried her into the cabin as he spoke and deposited her gently on the settee in the living room. "Now before we do anything else, let's have a look at that ankle of yours."

He removed her shoe gently. Her ankle was swollen and sore to touch, and as his fingers probed it gently, she tried not to wince. She still felt semi-dazed. It was like a dream that he was here, that they were safe inside together and that he was so concerned for her. And it was heaven simply to be looking at him. She didn't want to think further than that. She didn't want to know what had happened at the coast.

He straightened up at last. "I'm pretty sure you haven't broken any bones, but I'm going to get you to the doctor. . . . What's become of Paul Stanhope, by the way?"

She flushed guiltily. So he knew Paul and been here! "He—he left yesterday."

"Yesterday?" he repeated, and searched her eyes as if he were trying to decide whether she was telling the truth. "He didn't come back to Surfers Paradise."

"No. He said he'd go straight to Brisbane. He—he wanted me to go with him," she floundered, "but you said you'd be back today so I—I waited."

"Very considerate of you," he said, suddenly cold and withdrawn. "You can tell me all about it later—it's something we must talk about. But right now you'd better get out of those wet clothes. I'll help you to your room. Do you think you can manage to change, or do you want some assistance?"

"I can manage," she said quickly.

In her room, he insisted on putting out clean clothes for her and then to her relief he left her to herself, telling her, "When you're ready, I'm going to get you over to the coast so you can have that ankle attended to."

He disappeared, to change, too, she presumed. She wondered as she stripped off her wet things and got awkwardly into the clean underwear and the fuchsia pink dress he'd selected for her, how they could get to the coast since the road had collapsed. She puzzled over this problem, deliberately refusing to dwell on what he'd said about talking later—because she knew all too well what they were going to talk about, and just now she couldn't bear it.

Dressed, she hobbled across to the mirror. Her hair was beginning to dry and she combed it into shape, used her lipstick, and then went awkwardly back to the living room which was empty.

Steve, who'd changed his clothes, came in a few minutes later with a cup of tea and some biscuits.

"Get that inside you," he said, and vanished again.

By now, Carrie had decided he must be going to

get Alec Potter to drive them to where he'd left his car, or as near as possible, and she was right.

By the time he came back again, it had stopped raining, and soon she'd been installed in the back seat of Alec's car, while the two men sat in the front. The dirt track had been badly rutted by the storm, and Carrie was appalled when they finally reached the cut in the road and she saw what had happened. It had collapsed almost its whole width across, and a mass of debris had fallen over the edge into the gully. Steve's car was parked on the other side of the gaping hole, some distance back. Alec pulled up well away from the danger zone and Steve opened the door for Carrie and as she struggled out, lifted her in his arms. She made no protest, but let him carry her through the scrub on the high side of the road and to his car. Alec followed, bringing with him her luggage. So Steve had packed all her things while she drank her tea. And it meant that she wouldn't be coming back here again. Well, it was what she'd been expecting.

In his car beside him, she had nothing to say. She couldn't chatter when her heart was heavy, and he was silent, too. She'd been so elated when he'd found her in the rain forest, and now she was in the depths. She dreaded returning to the hotel apartment, meeting Janelle again. It would be better if she could stay with Kim. This segment of her life was a good as over, and she had to face the facts. She glanced at the man beside her, his unsmiling, intent profile, and she recalled fleetingly the moment when he'd found her and held her so tenderly, as if—

As if nothing, she told herself sharply, He'd just been normally thankful not to have a dead girl on his hands.

When they reached Surfers Paradise, and the Daystar Hotel, it was already dark, and to Carrie's relief, the apartment was empty. Janelle and Miss Higgins must have gone out, not expecting Steve to return tonight.

"You'd better get that foot up," Steve said, once they were inside. "Sit down on the couch—the long one—and I'll ring the doctor." He saw her settled, and then telephoned.

The doctor was there in ten minutes. He was a practical, cheerful man who examined her ankle carefully, taking his time, and finally pronouncing, as Steve had done, that there were no broken bones—but that it was a severe sprain. He bandaged her leg, told her to keep it up, suggested she should take aspirin and provided some anti-inflammatory tablets. Then, promising to call again, he left.

He'd no sooner gone than one of the waiters appeared with a dinner trolley, and Carrie realised she was hungry.

"We'll serve ourselves, Robert," Steve said, and the man left.

"Better eat in here," Steve suggested. "Then you can keep that foot up."

Carrie nodded. She felt nervous and on edge now that she was alone with Steve, and she wasn't looking forward to their talk, though possibly he'd hold it over till tomorrow, seeing she'd been injured. He helped her to veal and vegetables, and took a portion for himself, and as he sat down, she asked him uneasily, "When will Janelle and Miss Higgins be back?"

"They won't," he said abruptly, taking up his knife and fork. Carrie gave him a startled look and he went on, "They left for Quaama Springs shortly after I came back from Brisbane this morning. We had just enough time together for them to let me know that Paul Stanhope had gone up to see you and that he hadn't come back—and for me to discover that Nella had very obligingly told him how to find his way to my hideout," he concluded grimly.

Carrie didn't know quite what to make of that. She didn't know how long he'd been in Brisbane, and whether he and Janelle had talked before he went. And she didn't know if they'd made any sort of an agreement.

They continued eating in silence. Carrie let him help her to dessert—a simple mousse made with chestnut purée and decorated with a swirl of cream, and then she drank a small cup of black coffee. It wasn't till they'd quite finished and the waiter had come to remove their dishes that Steve got up from his chair, and pacing the floor restlessly told her almost harshly, "By the way, we're being married the day after tomorrow."

Carrie stared at him uncomprehendingly. Her heart seemed to stop for a moment and she felt herself go deathly pale. She'd been expecting to hear that he and Janelle were to be married. But—it was a strange way to tell her, his voice so hard and matter-of-fact, as if he were talking of something of no more importance than a visit to a restaurant or the dentist. Yet he'd said "we," her spinning senses suddenly pointed out. *We*. Did that mean—

She glanced up at him from under her lashes. He'd stopped his restless pacing and was standing, thumbs tucked into the waistband of his dark, hip-hugging pants, his blue gaze fixed on her.

"You mean," she began and stopped, her throat dry.

His eyes had narrowed. "Is it all that much of a shock to you? You can't have thought we'd put if off forever. I arranged it yesterday in Brisbane, before I heard you were entertaining your boyfriend up on the plateau. What were you hoping for when you waited around to see me, instead of disappearing with Paul?"

She flushed. "I—I thought you might tell me you didn't want to go on with it," she stammered.

His eyebrows rose sardonically. "Carrie, did I give you that impression during the time we spent together, getting to know each other?"

She shook her head. "It wasn't that. It was because of Quaama Springs."

"*Now* what are you talking about?" He came to sit on the edge of the sofa, far too close to her for comfort, his gaze fixed on her face.

She moved slightly. "Janelle told me about your father's will. She explained that if you and she don't marry, Quaama Springs will go to her." She took a deep breath and went on determinedly, somehow glad to be getting it all off her chest, "She said you'd disagreed about where you'd live when you were married and that you'd got engaged to me to make her give in. So I didn't think you meant to marry me at all, you see."

His mouth had tightened with anger. "Janelle's been telling you a pack of lies. I thought I made it clear to you the first day we met that I had no intention of marrying her. And I asked you to marry me for the reason I gave you then: I want a wife. And incidentally, to convince Janelle it was no use building plans around me. I discovered long ago that the fondness she'd always professed for Quaama Springs was mere pretence. She managed to influence my father in her favour. He let her stay on after her husband died and he did his best to persuade me to marry her. What she told you about his will was true—he favoured her in his will. And now you can forget all about Janelle, and remember just one thing—that I keep my promises, and when I make a plan I carry it out."

But you'll lose Quaama Springs, she wanted to say. She just couldn't understand it, especially when he'd said *one woman would do as well as another*. That was something she couldn't forget. She sank back on the sofa, closing her eyes. Janelle had been vanquished, but oh, if only it could have been different! If only he could have fallen in love with her as she had with him. Merely wanting a wife was hardly a good basis for a marriage.

She felt the movement of the sofa as he leaned nearer to her.

"Is your ankle painful, Carrie?" he asked, concern in his voice.

She shook her head. She'd forgotten all about her ankle. The pain was in her heart.

"Is it Paul?" he asked after a few seconds silence, and he no longer spoke gently. "You thought I was going to marry Janelle, and you'd be free to marry Paul. Well, you'll have to make up your mind it's going to be me, Carrie. It would really stick in my throat to pay off your boyfriend's debts and then hand you back to him afterwards."

Carrie's eyes flew open. "My boyfriend's debts?" she repeated blankly.

"Well, aren't they?" he said dryly. "You insisted they were yours, but from your reaction when I questioned you the other day it was obvious you were lying. And don't forget I read your letter. Paul was looking for someone to make him a loan and Carrie Adams had raced off to the Gold Coast to find a gullible millionaire. Well, you found me, and for you that's the end of the line."

She shook her head dazedly. "It wasn't like that. I only made a joke about coming to the Gold Coast to find a millionaire when—when Paul and I broke up. I really came here because of Kim. Oh, I suppose I'll have to tell you now, it doesn't matter so much since she's going to be married and will be leaving the hotel." She looked up at him, her dark eyes wide and anxious. "It was Kim who was in trouble. It's her debt, not Paul's."

"What?" She saw the sharp shock of surprise in his eyes. "Good heavens! Kim—with her cute little-girl face—spilling out her sobstory of a spendthrift cousin on my shoulder! I can't believe it!"

"She didn't mean any harm," Carrie said quickly. "She was frightened she'd get the sack, go to gaol. She knew about Aunt Lena's legacy and there was no one else she could turn to but me. You see, her father was a hopeless gambler, and Aunt Janet had a full-time job, and me to look after as well as Kim—she just didn't have the time to give Kim the love or the sense of security a child needs. That's why—"

"Spare me the excuses," he broke in. "It was immoral of Kim to do what she did, to lie to me about you, to—" He broke off and looked at Carrie thoughtfully. "It's thanks to Kim we met, I suppose."

"Yes," she said, puzzled by his expression.

"And it's Kim who owes me six thousand dollars."

"No it's not," she said at once. "It's me—I agreed to settle her debt. I'll pay you back the money."

184

He raised his eyebrows. "No, you won't, Carrie. You're going to marry me, as we arranged. You're not going to run out on me—not for any reason."

She stared at him. It wasn't as though he loved her. It was his terrible pride. Once he'd been jilted, he wasn't going to let that happen again.

She said shakily, "You can break it off this time, Steve."

"What on earth's that supposed to mean?"

"I know you were jilted once," she said unwillingly. "I know that's why you're so—so heartless and callous."

His mouth twisted. "Is that how you see me? I wasn't jilted, as a matter of fact. The girl I was going to marry had a lover in the background. She planned to have the best of two worlds. When I found out about it, I told her not to turn up at the church. That, and the fact that I've been immersed in work for the past few years, have kept me from thinking seriously of marriage again. Until now."

Their eyes met for a burning second, and then she turned her face away from him. "I can't marry you," she said huskily. "I want to marry for love." Suddenly she was on the edge of tears. "My ankle's painful. I'd like to go to bed."

She sat up and put her feet to the floor and he stood up and reached out his arms to her.

"I'll get you some aspirin," he said, his voice strained. "Let me help you into your room."

She drew back from him. The thought of having him touch her was too much. "Leave me alone. I can manage."

He said nothing, but she felt his eyes following her as she made her way slowly and awkwardly across the carpeted floor.

It was strange to be back in the big bedroom she'd been given when first she came here. It seemed an age ago, so much had happened since then. Despite her ankle, she went to the big windows and stood looking out at the night. There had been rain at the coast, but now in the darkness of night the sea was calm and flat. Its assaults on the shore had quietened down to a playful running and retreating, and she could hear only a gentle hush-hush sound instead of the continuous roar she had become accustomed to.

She stood staring out across the narrow balcony, but presently she was seeing nothing. She was thinking. *What's wrong with me? I could marry him if I wanted. I have only to say yes. Even if he doesn't love me, I'll be his wife, I'll sleep in his bed, in his arms.* But she knew her heart would ache for something she couldn't have. And besides, mightn't the time come when he'd regret that he hadn't married Janelle, and kept possession of his beloved Quaama Springs? After all, one woman was the same as another to him. She couldn't understand it, that he was intent on marrying her. Was it just a sort of stubborn pride in keeping his promises?

She turned back into the room. No, she couldn't do it. Some day, years and years into the future when she'd managed to forget Steve, she might meet another man she could love—a man who would love her, too.

Her bags had been unpacked, all her clothes put away, probably by one of the housemaids while she and Steve were dining, and laid out on the bed was one of the lovely nightgowns Steve had bought for her in Brisbane—a rose gown made of the softest satin. She took it up and went into the pretty bathroom that opened off her room, where she showered refreshingly, but with difficulty. She had just come back and got under the sheet when Steve knocked at the door and came in. He had a glass of milk in one hand and an aspirin bottle in the other.

"This will help you sleep," he said, coming across the room to the bed.

Carrie sat up against the pillows. Something drastic seemed to happen to her will at the very sight of him. How could she not marry him when that was what he wanted? She watched him put the glass down on the bedside table, open the bottle and shake two tablets into his hand. Then he raised his head and their eyes met. His glance moved to her mouth, then to her breast, palpitating slightly under the soft satin of the gown, then returned to her eyes. A shock went through her, straight to her heart, and she felt herself tremble. Why not say yes, and forget all the complications, all the doubts?

He sat down on the side of the bed and asked abruptly, his blue eyes curiously dark, "What did you mean when you said that, Carrie?"

"Said what?" she asked bewildered.

"That you wanted to marry for love." She said nothing and he asked tensely, "Have you made up with Paul? Do you want to marry him?"

She bit her lip. "It's all over."

Their glances clung and then he took her two hands in his and pulled her to him, crushing her against his breast, touching her mouth gently with his own. Fire ran along her nerves and she felt her whole being go limp as the touch of his lips resolved itself into a kiss that was both tender and fiercely passionate. All her tensions vanished and she gave way to her feelings completely, clinging to him, kissing him back.

When at last he let her go, he said softly, "You love me, Carrie, don't you?"

"Yes," she said brokenly. It was no use denying it, and she drew away from him tremblingly, feeling ashamed.

He pushed the hair back from her face with a touch that was tender. "Then marry me," he said. "I want to marry for love, too."

She looked up at him, startled by something in his tone. Their eyes met, and his weren't enigmatic anymore. There was an expression in them that made her go limp all over again.

"But you said one woman would do as well as another," she said huskily, unable to look away from him.

"I know I did." He took her hand in his and gently rubbed his thumb across her palm. "I've changed my mind since I met you. I never thought it would happen to me, Heaven knows, but it has. I love you, Carrie. I guess I knew it long ago though I wouldn't admit it. I was hellishly jealous when you got that letter from Paul. I could see history repeating itself, see myself married to a wife with a lover in the background—but even then I was determined to have you, I knew I wouldn't let you go. And when I saw you lying face down on the ground today—and I thought you were dead—" He stopped, his voice hoarse with emotion. "I knew then what it was all about. I love you, Carrie. You matter more than anything in the world to me."

"More than—Quaama Springs?" she asked, half-crying but somehow half-laughing, too.

"Oh the devil with Quaama Springs," he said. "Janelle will put it up for sale. If you like it, if you want to taste country life, we'll buy it."

He took her in his arms once more and when he'd kissed her breathless he murmured, "I suppose we should put off our wedding. You'll want to wait till you can float down the aisle like a true bride."

She shook her head, clinging to him fiercely. "I don't want to wait, Steve. So long as it's you waiting for me at the other end."

"I'll be waiting," he promised and they were in each other's arms again.

Silhouette **Romance**

15-Day Free Trial Offer
6 Silhouette Romances

6 Silhouette Romances, free for 15 days! We'll send you 6 new Silhouette Romances to keep for 15 days, absolutely free! If you decide not to keep them, send them back to us. You pay nothing.

Free Home Delivery. But if you enjoy them as much as we think you will, keep them by paying the invoice enclosed with your free trial shipment. We'll pay all shipping and handling charges. You get the convenience of Home Delivery and we pay the postage and handling charge each month.

Don't miss a copy. The Silhouette Book Club is the way to make sure you'll be able to receive every new romance we publish before they're sold out. There is no minimum number of books to buy and you can cancel at any time.

This offer expires February 28, 1982

Silhouette Book Club, Dept. **SBG**17B
120 Brighton Road, Clifton, NJ 07012

Please send me 6 Silhouette Romances to keep for 15 days, absolutely free. I understand I am not obligated to join the Silhouette Book Club unless I decide to keep them.

NAME_____

ADDRESS_____

CITY_____STATE_____ZIP_____